ENTICED BY THE ALIEN WARRIOR

HOPE HART

The Arcav Alien Invasion Series

The Arcav King's Mate

The Arcav Commander's Human

The Arcav General's Woman

The Arcav Prince's Captive

A Very Arcav Christmas

The Arcav Captain's Queen

The Arcav Guard's Female

The Warriors of Agron Series

Taken by the Alien Warrior

Claimed by the Alien Warrior

Saved by the Alien Warrior

Seduced by the Alien Warrior

Protected by the Alien Warrior

Captured by the Alien Warrior

Rescued by the Alien Warrior

Enticed by the Alien Warrior

Conquered by the Alien Warrior

The Society of Savages Series

Wicked

Depraved

Brutal

CHAPTER ONE

Vivian

*W*e're *defined by our actions. By the things we do when no one is watching. By the way we behave when we're only accountable to ourselves.*

But most importantly, we're defined by the steps we take when saving ourselves means harm to someone else.

What do you do when your back is against the wall?

Either way, I will be forever defined by the choice I'm about to make. And there's one thing that no one tells you about those difficult, life-defining actions. Others may judge you, but they get to walk away. You're the one who has to live with yourself.

Arix

I watch the small human females as they walk toward my castle. Vivian smiles, and I can't help but stare. From the moment my eyes met hers so many days ago, I was entranced. Her beauty makes her seem cool, almost icy, but I have no doubt that beneath the composure she wears like a mask is a female who burns with the hottest blue flame.

"I don't like this," Korzyn murmurs. "I don't trust them."

I glance over my shoulder at where my commander is leaning against the wall, his eyes also on the two human females.

"You don't trust anyone."

He shrugs. "That may be true, but I especially don't trust females who may have been planted here by your enemies. You have no true alliance with the barbarians across the water. What if they have been sent here to gather intelligence and report back?"

I wave a hand, turning back to where Vivian is throwing her head back with laughter at something the other female says. I have a sudden urge to lean out the window so I can hear the sound.

"What intelligence can they gather? I've assigned guards to them, and they won't be walking around the castle unattended."

"What if they're here to kill you?"

As the females move into the castle and out of my view, I sigh, turning back to the male who has been staunchly at my side since the day my parents died and I picked up my father's crown.

"You believe those tiny females could kill me?"

His frown deepens. "They could be used as a distraction."

There have been numerous attempts on my life over the years. While my parents' deaths are officially considered to be accidents, I know the truth.

They were cold-blooded murders. And I was supposed to be the third victim, leaving my throne up for grabs.

As much as I tease Korzyn for his paranoia, there's no question that that paranoia has kept me alive more times than I can count. And if he has a bad feeling…

"I'll be careful," I say. "I swear it."

All these years, and I still haven't discovered who killed my parents. I have discovered traitors, of course. One of my first orders as king was the execution of the guard who was supposed to be by my parents' side that night but was found attempting to escape my kingdom.

But I've never found the person responsible for making me king before my time. The thought of my revenge is the first thing that crosses my mind when I open my eyes in the morning and the last thing when I close them at night.

My gaze clings to Vivian's face as I push the thought of my parents away. I want the little human. I've wanted her since the moment I laid my eyes on her. She's beautiful and brave, and something about the way she holds herself makes me think she might be broken.

Like me.

But that's all this is. I want to lose myself in her body, cut myself on her sharp edges. I want to roll her across my sheets and spread her hair along my pillow. And then, when I am finished with her, I will kiss her goodbye and send her on her way when she leaves my planet. Forever.

Vivian

My stomach is tense as Sarissa and I hug Zoey goodbye.

"Are you sure about this?" she asks again as Hewex and Tagiz frown disapprovingly.

I throw them a wink. "Positive."

She looks doubtful, but if I'm going in, I'm going all in.

Sarissa raises her eyebrow at me, but she picks up what I'm throwing at her, giving Zoey a wide smile.

"This is an excellent idea. We'll be in touch as soon as we've gotten this part fixed."

Tagiz practically has to drag Zoey away, but she finally gives us one last hug, and my cousin and I are suddenly alone on the "other" side of the Colossal Water.

I slide Sarissa a look. "This was a smart decision, right?" I ask.

My cousin shrugs. "Girl, I was just going along with whatever plan you'd cooked up."

I narrow my eyes at her, and she grins, nudging me with her shoulder. "I'm not saying it's a bad plan, just that I practically got whiplash from your decision-making process."

I sigh. Okay, so I may have a rather large chip on my shoulder about contributing to the cause. I've spent most of my time on Agron being a distraction while the other women got shit done. Now it's my turn to help us get our ship fixed so we can finally get off this planet.

Not that this planet is bad. It's barbaric, that's for sure, although the Braxians have treated us like family since the moment Rakiz's tribe rescued us. But when you're plucked from your life without any warning, you'll do just about anything to get that life back.

"Well," I say as we turn and follow the guards toward the giant obsidian castle, "decision made. No turning back now."

We have a lead on someone who can fix the thruster from our ship, but apparently the guy only visits Agron sporadically. Hence why we're here.

Arix—the king on this side of the Colossal Water—has

already left to do whatever it is he does. For now, his guards are going to show us to our rooms.

Rooms. In a castle.

Yeah, whiplash is right. Before this, we were sleeping in kradis—comfortable, clean tents, but tents just the same. This is a life upgrade, although I already miss the other women. Nevada and Ellie are both pregnant and due to pop any day, and I've become close with Zoey and even a few of the new human women who were trapped in a cage on the ship full of Dokhalls that attempted to take us back.

We leave the dock behind and enter the castle from the back, clomping up the black stone steps and along silver tiles that are so polished I can see my reflection in them. Our footsteps echo as we file down the hallway until we're back in the main entrance hall. I can't help but gaze up.

There are some places that make you feel small. The Grand Canyon. The redwood parks in California. The open ocean.

This castle is like that.

It's made of some kind of black stone, but the word *black* doesn't do it justice. It's so dark that it seems to absorb the light, reflecting it back in the gleaming veins of silver that peek out here and there.

It would be gloomy and depressing if not for the massive windows above us, providing the natural light throughout the hall.

One of the guards clears his throat, and I glance at Sarissa. Both of us are standing here with our mouths open as we examine the entrance hall. I laugh.

"We're like a couple of small-town girls in the big city for the first time," I mutter, and she grins.

We follow the guards up the massive staircase, which leads to a landing. Above us, more corridors intersect, cutting through the air above and below one another in a dizzying pattern. People are hurrying down those corridors, a few of them glancing at us curiously, but they've obviously got places to go because no one pauses.

By the time the guards stop outside a silver door, I'm completely and utterly lost, and I can tell by the tiny line between Sarissa's eyebrows that she feels the same.

"Do you guys have some kind of map we can use while we're here?" she asks.

The guard smiles, but it doesn't reach his eyes. "We will escort you anywhere you need to go."

Sarissa and I share a glance. Arix referred to us as his guests. But if he expects guards to be with us each time we leave our rooms, it seems we're really more like prisoners.

She nods, a silent agreement that we'll discuss this later. The guard opens the door and gestures her in, and he stays behind to show her through the room, while another guard opens the next door down for me.

At least we'll be close to each other.

"This is your sitting room, and through that door, you'll find your bathing room." He strides to the right, opening another door. "Bedroom. Please pull the cord by the door if you need anything and a servant will come to help you."

The suite is gorgeous. I wander into the bedroom, my mouth gaping at the size of the bed. A vanity sits by an open closet, and I frown.

"Is this someone else's room?"

The guard tilts his head. "I'm not sure what you mean."

"The clothes..."

"They're for you."

I feel a little like Alice, and I've just fallen down the rabbit hole. I stride to the closet and pull out one of the dresses. It looks like it'll fit perfectly. But Arix had no way of knowing we'd stay here. Did he?

"Thank you," I murmur, and the guard nods, backing out of the room.

Moments later, Sarissa appears, nodding at the dress I'm still holding. "It's weird, huh?"

"Braxian women are so much taller than us. It's like he had these dresses made in advance."

"I've said it before, and I'll say it again. I don't trust him."

Sarissa works for the CIA. And no, I have no idea what she does. She clams up every time I ask about it, so I'm pretty sure she's not allowed to talk about what her day-to-day tasks actually are.

I blow out a breath. "Look, no matter his reasons for wanting us here, we know why *we* want to be here. If we can get the thruster fixed and find someone to replace that chip...we could be out of here within a few weeks. Let's keep our eye on the prize."

Sarissa nods, wandering over to my bed and running her hand over the ruby-red velvet blanket draped over the end. "I'll get to work on an escape plan," she murmurs, "just in case."

CHAPTER TWO

V ivian

I stare into the mirror, poking at one of the dark circles beneath my eyes. I was so tired last night that I thought I'd pass out before my head hit the pillow. Instead, I tossed and turned, unable to sleep properly without the gentle murmur of the camp around me.

I finally snuck out of my room and into Sarissa's, ignoring the guards posted in the hall. I hadn't even made it into her bedroom before she appeared, eyes hard, a knife clutched in her hand.

She let out a long breath when our eyes met, glancing down at the knife in her hand apologetically. I merely revealed the knife in my own hand, hidden by the folds of the nightgown I was wearing.

Sarissa smirked. "Proud of you, V."

We spent the rest of the night huddled next to each other in her huge bed, whispering like kids. Eventually, I fell into a light, continually broken sleep, and I finally gave up when the room began to lighten as the sun rose.

I reach for a cool cloth and press it against my eyes in an attempt to remove some of the puffiness. I can barely throw a punch, but I've managed to master the no-makeup look on a barbaric alien planet.

I snort, disgusted with myself.

I know what people think when they look at me. They see a pretty face but not much between the ears. They see decoration. A ditz. Someone who's only good at looking good.

I guess that's why I came to Arix in the first place. I was so sick of being left behind every time. I may not be creating poisons like Zoey or hunting the enemy from on top of a dragon like Charlie, but this is a way *I* can contribute.

That's the thing about playing a part. When you pretend to be someone different, it's easy to lose sight of who you really are. Eventually, you become that new person, and before you know it, there's nothing left of the person you were.

I don't know who I am anymore.

I jump at a knock on the door. Sarissa wouldn't knock, and I glance down at the nightgown and robe I'm wearing. Once, when I was a teenager, I opened the front door while still in my pajamas on a Sunday morning. My mother was so furious she couldn't look at me for days.

I push the thoughts away. I haven't spoken to my mother for years. So why am I suddenly being assaulted by thoughts about what she would think of me right now?

I march to the door and throw it open, expecting to see one of the guards.

It's not.

It's the king.

He stands there, looking coolly amused as I gape at him. Finally, he must get tired of my fish impression because he raises one eyebrow.

"May I come in?"

"Um. Sure."

The room instantly feels five times smaller as soon as Arix enters it. The guy is one of the largest Braxians I've ever seen, and he holds himself with a kind of languid confidence that falls perilously close to arrogance.

His eyes are the color of a moonlit night sky, the kind of deep, unfathomable blue that makes it difficult to look away. Full black brows frame those eyes, contrasting with the wild blue. His dark hair matches the brows, curling around his shoulders and bringing out the glow of his skin in a way that makes him look like a fallen angel.

The first time I saw him, my breath caught in my throat. The second time, I almost lost the ability to speak a full sentence. Now I feel a blush begin to rise, and I step back, my stomach twisting.

I don't understand what happens to my body when this guy is around. I'm never affected by men. At least, not in this way.

"How are you settling in?" he asks, and I almost shiver at his low voice.

"Fine, thank you. The rooms are beautiful."

He glances around the sitting room as if he's never seen it before but immediately returns his attention to my face.

I squirm under his regard. "Why are you looking at me like that?"

Surprise flashes across his face. "You're beautiful," he says. "Why wouldn't I enjoy looking at you?"

Disappointment burns in my belly, even as I attempt a smile. I don't know what I was expecting. This guy doesn't know me, doesn't know *anything* about me. So why would I hope he was interested in more than just the face I happened to be born with?

"I've upset you."

"No." Just confirmed my expectations.

"Don't lie to me."

I change the subject instead. "Is there something I can help you with?"

"Yes," he says. "I want to tumble you."

Arix

Vivian's mouth drops open in a way that makes me imagine her swallowing my cock, and I force my attention elsewhere. I stride toward the window, gazing down at the gardens below as I give her the moment she obviously needs to recover.

"Excuse me?" Her voice is strangled, and I glance over my shoulder, pleased to find her face flushed, even if her eyes are narrowed in a way that suggests she's thinking about doing me harm.

"I didn't realize humans were so hard of hearing," I say, just so I can see her eyes blaze. For some reason, watching this female lose her composure makes me harder than I've ever been in my life.

"I heard you," she snaps. "I just thought maybe you had some kind of brain fart and didn't actually mean to say that to me."

I give her my most charming grin. She doesn't seem impressed. "I never say things I don't mean. Life is too short."

"Uh-huh. And what makes you think I'd want to 'tumble' you?"

I turn my back to the window and raise one eyebrow. Perhaps she hasn't properly examined me. I open my arms wide so she can appreciate every inch of my body, sending her a wink as she snorts in disdain.

She curls her lip at me, and it takes every drop of my self-control not to stride across the room and plunder her mouth.

It's not just her beauty that makes me almost desperate to tumble this female. It's the fire I can see burning within her. The fire she keeps carefully banked, hidden away where she thinks no one can see it.

But I can.

I have no doubt that beneath her cool exterior is a female who burns with passion.

She pretends indifference. "You're hot. So what?"

I smile at her, and her lip twitches. Aha! She *does* find me charming.

"No other warrior has claimed you, lovely."

Something I can't place flashes across her face. "What exactly are you implying?"

"Nothing. I'm telling you that you were meant to be mine. For as long as you're on this planet and while you're organizing your trip home," I clarify, so she'll understand I have no intention of claiming her long-term.

"Uh-huh," she says again, and my abs tighten. Something about the way this female pretends to be unimpressed with me makes me want to bend her over and make her scream my name. "Look, I appreciate the offer," she says, as if she's refusing another course at dinner, "but I'm not really on the lookout for a 'tumble.'"

"And that's entirely why you need one," I tell her. "You

have a lot to do if you're going to get off this planet. You'll think more clearly after a few nights in my bed."

She blinks. "Did you just offer to fuck the focus into me?"

I shrug. "If you're going to leave this planet, don't you want to experience all it has to offer?"

"Now you're making it sound like your cock is the eighth wonder of Agron." She rolls her eyes.

"I don't know what the eight wonders are," I say. "But my cock would definitely be wonder number one."

"You're insane."

I shrug. "You and I both know this is going to happen. It's just a matter of *when*. How much time do you want to waste before I make you come harder than you've ever come before in your life?"

She studies me. While she's feigning boredom, I've spent my life negotiating with council members and leaders from across Agron. I know reluctant interest when I see it.

She opens her mouth, and I frown at a knock on the door. I made it clear I wasn't to be disturbed.

"You should put some clothes on."

"Excuse me?"

This again. "Perhaps humans really are hard of hearing." I wave my hand, gesturing to her robe. "No one will see you in your nightclothes except me."

She grinds her teeth, then strides to the door and flings it open before I can stop her. I'm going to bend this female over my knees and give her a good spanking. She obviously needs it.

I stalk toward her, pulling her behind me, but it's just Bevix—one of my advisers and closest friends. I left instructions that I was only to be disturbed in an emergency, and I can tell by the look in his eyes that another attack has happened.

I grind my teeth. "Vivian, this is Bevix."

To Bevix's credit, his eyes may light with interest when he looks at Vivian, but they immediately clear when he glances back at my face. He has always been quick.

Bevix nods hello at Vivian, who moves away, wrapping her gauzy robe more tightly around her.

"Korzyn asks you to come to him immediately," he says, eyes flicking between me and Vivian. He's being careful not to say anything she could pass to others, obviously on Korzyn's orders, and I nod, glancing over my shoulder at Vivian.

"We will talk about this later, lovely."

Vivian

I throw myself on Sarissa's bed, and she raises her eyebrow at me as she leans back against her stack of pillows.

"What's going on?"

"Arix said he wants me."

Sarissa smirks. "And that's somehow news to you?"

I run my hand over the velvet throw at the end of her bed, and she sighs.

"Do you want him?"

I keep my eyes on the lush dark-red blanket. "Maybe."

She nudges me with her foot. "Do I need to sit on you and tickle you until you tell me what I need to know?"

I laugh, finally meeting her eyes. Sarissa has always been stronger than me, and she used to torture me by tickling me when we were kids. If she was really mad, she'd hold me down and spit in my hair.

I may have been younger and smaller, but I always retaliated in the sneakiest way possible. Once I dyed her hair black while she was asleep. Of course, I could only reach certain spots without waking her, and her pillowcase was ruined, but the look on her face when she caught a glimpse of herself in the mirror was worth the icy lecture from my mother and the inevitable grounding from my father.

She eyes me. "What are you thinking about?"

"That time I dyed your hair. You looked like a skunk."

She glowers at me, but we both burst out laughing. "My mom nearly killed you."

"You deserved it. It's your own fault for sleeping like the dead."

She laughs, and I chew on my lip.

"Arix is probably just playing with me."

Sarissa opens her mouth, but I'm already climbing off the bed. She snaps her mouth closed and shrugs. "I've arranged for the guards to take us back to the marketplace today," she says.

"I thought that woman said her contact wasn't arriving for a few weeks?"

"True, but I want to get to know the lay of the land. Plus, if we sniff around for long enough, we might get lucky and find someone who can help us find a replacement for that chip."

According to Alexis, our ship is run almost entirely by artificial intelligence. And while the electronic systems all work together, it's unlikely we'll be going anywhere without the control chip, which is about the size of a SIM card.

There's a chance that Alexis can figure out a way for us to get out of here without the chip, and while a few of the other women are willing to take the chance, most of us are attached to our lives and don't like the idea of being blown apart in space.

Unfortunately, whichever Dokhall was piloting that ship was a step ahead of us, and he took the chip with him. If we knew who had it, we could try to negotiate with him, but with our luck, it's likely he was one of the many creatures Dragix turned to ash in the last battle.

Sarissa stretches. "If we can find a replacement, most of our problems will be solved. Plus, we have Kate."

My stomach twists in both fear and anticipation. I want to get off Agron, but obviously, none of us has ever flown a spaceship before. Kate is one of the women who landed when the Dokhalls attempted to take us back. On Earth, she was a test pilot for a private company developing space planes for tourism before the Arcav invaded. Once the Arcav shut down the skies, that project was a bust. But she's still the most obvious person for the job.

Unfortunately, she's not all that interested in taking the job. Last time we chatted, she glanced around the clearing at all the other women who want to leave Agron, and her face hardened. "Would you want to be responsible for all these lives?" she asked. "If Alexis can prove to me that the AI system can basically fly the ship itself, I'll do it. But I'm not about to take everyone else down with me."

Sarissa nudges me, and I blink.

"Sorry, I was thinking about Kate."

She nods. "She's a lone wolf, that woman. Without the chip, she's likely to put her foot down. Even with the chip, it's going to take all our considerable charm to convince her to take the job."

I laugh at that. Most of the time, Sarissa has about as much charm as a quarterback who just lost the Superbowl.

But there's no question that she can still turn it on when she needs to.

"I'm going to go get ready," I say.

When I open my door, a random woman is waiting for me, and I jolt.

"Uh, hi."

She runs critical eyes over me. "Not yet dressed at this hour of the day? And your hair not even combed?"

Shame makes my shoulders hunch, and the familiar feel of it pisses me off.

"And just who are you?"

"Your maid."

"I don't need a maid."

She runs dark eyes over me, the look of disdain reminding me of my mother.

"Clearly," she says, "you do."

"I can dress myself. Leave."

"The king ordered me to provide you with the help you so obviously need. I take my orders from him."

I grind my teeth. "Fine." I'll deal with her today and take this up with Arix next time I see him. I don't need to be humiliated first thing in the morning. "What's your name?"

"Cauri. Hurry up, your bath is waiting."

I scowl at her but roll my eyes, padding into the bathroom. As I slip into the warm water, I imagine Sarissa dealing with a lady's maid, and the thought makes me grin.

"Out, out, we don't have all day," Cauri says.

"What are you talking about?"

"You will go to the marketplace with the other human woman." Her brow creases in obvious disapproval, and I wonder if she was eavesdropping.

I scowl. Arix and I will have words, oh yes we will.

I get out of the bath at her urging, wrapping a large cloth

around myself. She points toward my bedroom, where I step into a dress of her choosing, muttering under my breath.

The dress is a light-pink color, with silver thread woven through it. It's pretty enough, but my cleavage is poking up higher than even I'm used to.

I like playing dress-up—it's my job on Earth after all—but the gown Cauri is currently tightening until I can barely take a full breath...

"This seems a little over the top for a trip to the market."

"You're staying with the king. You represent him now."

I roll my eyes again but suck in a breath as she tightens the strings even more.

"Tiny waist," she says approvingly. If I roll my eyes any more, they're likely to get stuck up there.

"Sit down so I can do your hair."

I comply. "Aren't maids supposed to *take* orders? Ow!"

She pulls my hair, and I glare at her reflection in the mirror. Her expression is mild, but I huff. She definitely did that on purpose.

The familiar feeling of sitting in front of a mirror while someone does my hair...it makes my stomach clench.

When I was a kid, I briefly thought I was going to be a doctor. My nanny once read me a book about different careers, and I told my mother I was going to help sick people. But my mother killed those illusions. And over the years, she set fire to them and buried them.

"Darling, you're too pretty to be locked away in a lab," she cooed. "You need to do something that will show off that gorgeous face."

I was four.

My mother got to work, and within a few weeks, I had an agent. Within a few months, I was doing commercials.

Within a few years, I was modeling in a kids' runway show in Paris.

My mother was ecstatic.

My stomach rumbles, and I force myself to push the memories away.

"I'm hungry. Where can I get breakfast around here?"

Cauri waves her hand toward a tray I hadn't noticed on a small table near my bed. My stomach rumbles again, and I tense, ready to ditch the maid and leap on the food like a hungry wildebeest.

She tugs at my hair again. "Don't even think about it."

"Ow!"

I glare at her. I spent hours of my life sitting in front of mirrors being painted and prodded. I'm not putting up with it on this planet.

"Enough."

She must realize she's dancing on my last nerve, because she slides one final pin into my hair and pronounces me ready to go.

I may dislike this woman, but habit—and manners—kick in.

"Thank you."

Surprise flashes across her face, and she nods, pointing toward my breakfast.

"Eat," she says and then stalks out of my room.

I would've killed for a maid in Rakiz's camp. Now I have one, and she's a dictator. Just my luck.

CHAPTER THREE

A rix

Another of my most trusted guards is dead with no warning. My hands fist as I stare down at his body. Heril was a good male. One who guarded me loyally after the deaths of my parents.

"How?" I murmur.

Bevix leans down and pulls aside Heril's black uniform, revealing the wound.

"Stabbed in the heart," Korzyn mutters behind me. "Quick, lethal, and done by someone he trusted enough to let them get that close."

And that makes it so much worse. Over the past revolution, many of my most trusted guards have been killed, one by one, leaving me with an increasingly sparse group of those I can trust. Someone wants my throne. And they are getting impatient.

"I want to visit his family."

Bevix nods. "I will make arrangements."

How will I face Heril's mate, Caris? How will I face his parents, knowing it is my fault he is lying here, killed by someone he trusted? By someone *I* trusted.

Korzyn slaps his hand on my shoulder. "We *will* find who did this," he murmurs. "And we will make them pay."

I nod, feeling as if I am in a daze as I make my way to my throne room. I have a meeting with my advisers, who are debating the merits of creating potential trade agreements with some of the barbarian Braxian tribes from across the water. My spies are currently closely watching the tribes' qatais, judging how likely they would be to honor any potential alliances.

"Arix," my uncle booms as I walk into the empty room. Behind me, I can practically hear Korzyn grinding his teeth. My commander is convinced that Tridi is responsible for these attacks. As I have no heirs, my uncle would be the next in line for my throne.

However, even with all Korzyn's spies and his constant, continual monitoring of Tridi, he has never been able to provide any evidence that the other male is responsible for my parents' murders.

Each time I see my uncle, I fight the urge to order him to leave my court. Not just because the chance he is betraying me is high but because his face is so close to my father's that my gut sometimes twists when I look at him. My father would have those lines beside his eyes now. Would likely have the beginnings of gray in his hair.

"Tridi." I take my throne, watching as his eyes flare at the sight.

"What's this I hear about human females staying as your *guests*?"

I raise one eyebrow. I have no obligation to explain

myself to Tridi, but since he's a council member, it's often best to placate him.

"They wish to use contacts within the marketplace to fix their ship."

Bevix is leaning against one of the walls, and his eyes widen. The male has long been fascinated with the idea of traveling between planets, and I have no doubt he will want to speak with the human females.

I bite down the urge to warn him that while he may speak to Sarissa, Vivian is off-limits. No. Even if she does take me up on my offer, I don't become possessive of females. My focus is entirely on ruling my kingdom and avenging my parents' deaths.

I glance at Korzyn, and he nods. Just as my enemies have spies in this court, I do. Just as they are getting closer to taking my throne, I am getting closer to discovering exactly who they are.

And when I find out who is responsible for so much death...

They will pay.

Vivian

I crunch down on a nut as Sarissa and I wander through the marketplace. Since we're not strolling around with Arix this time, the people here barely pay us any attention. We've convinced the guards to follow us at a distance, and we're squeezing through the crowded space, occasionally elbowing each other as we notice something that grabs our attention.

And almost everything grabs our attention.

The kradis are three-sided, and vendors—both from Agron and across the galaxy—are displaying their wares and negotiating with buyers. The air vibrates with the sounds of laughing, haggling, and so many languages that the translator in my ear is likely working harder than it ever has.

A man with hooves clomps toward a vendor selling jewelry, and I fight not to stare as he scans the display. Beside me, Sarissa is tense, one hand buried in her dress, likely clutching the handle of her knife. Her other hand is wrapped around the broken piece of the thruster. While we have a lead on someone who can replace it for us, there's no harm in seeing if any of the other vendors here can get the job done more quickly.

"You know what I was thinking?" I ask, and she glances at me before quickly returning her attention to the crowd surrounding us.

"What?"

"This is the most time we've spent together in years."

She smiles. "Yeah. I'm always out of the country for work. And when I'm home, you're posing on a beach somewhere."

I flinch at that, and of course she notices. "I'm not being bitchy, V. You're one of the hardest-working people I know."

I smile, but it feels fake on my face. While I don't know exactly what Sarissa does, she's constantly traveling. Either way, she's helping to keep our country safe, while I'm helping brands sell their bikinis.

"Step right up, hit the target, and win a prize."

I blink at that, and we both turn to a small stall. "What is this, a carnival?" I ask.

This kradi is larger than most, and at the end, opposite

us, a target has been set up. It's small and seems to be hanging rather precariously in place.

Along the front of the stall, a crowd is beginning to gather, a man with light-purple skin picking up a small wrapped bag.

He growls as he hefts it in his hand. "This has been weighted."

The vendor, a Braxian woman, smiles at him. "The challenge is what makes the win worth it."

Sarissa nudges me. "Go on, use your superpower to win us a prize."

I roll my eyes. My "superpower" is a party trick I used to pull out to impress guys I liked, usually while playing darts after a few drinks. I can't catch a ball to save my life, but I have an unerring ability to hit almost everything I aim at. I was pretty good with a crossbow during our battle with the Dokhalls, but I really shine when it comes to throwing things.

"What do we get if we win?"

Sarissa frowns at me. "The knowledge that we won, of course. Who cares about the prize; think about your reputation."

I roll my eyes. My cousin is the most competitive person I've ever met. No one would play board games with her when we were kids, and she still has the uncanny ability to turn almost anything into a competition.

Sarissa is practically vibrating beside me. "Look, I'd do it, but my aim is crap compared to yours. Besides," she says, lowering her voice, "this is a good way to get to know the locals. Locals who may be able to help us in the future, you know what I mean?"

I sigh. Trust Sarissa to be thinking three steps ahead.

"Fine."

The purple man misses the target completely, his cheeks darkening as the crowd jeers. He stomps off, not looking back, and I step into the line behind a blue guy with thick horns sticking up from his head.

He hits the very edge of the target, hands over some credits for another shot, and then misses.

My turn.

"Come on, cuz. Don't let me down."

I give her a look, but she's already scanning the crowd. I have no idea what her endgame is. Perhaps it really is about us winning something in front of all these people.

"Tiny female." A male snorts behind us. "No chance."

I ignore him, but next to me, Sarissa glances over her shoulder.

"Opinions are like assholes," she says. "Everyone has one, but they're mostly full of shit."

He frowns as he ponders that, and I heft the small bag into my hand. The other guy was right. It is weighted. I shrug, haul my arm back, and throw.

It hits a hair's breadth from the target, and the crowd gasps. Sarissa shrugs. "A few first-time nerves," she says, handing over more credits.

She slaps me on the shoulder. "Don't let me down."

I can't help but laugh. "You're ridiculous, you know that?"

"Yeah, yeah. Hit the bull's-eye or you're walking home."

I roll my eyes but pick up another bag. Now I'm feeling the thrill of competition myself. And I'm having...fun. How long has it been since I did something just for the fun of it?

I let the bag fly, and a grin spreads across my face before I can stop it, satisfaction burning deep in my belly as I hit the center of the target.

Sarissa whoops and throws her arms around me. "I'm so

glad your superpower came through and I don't have to disown you. Let's see what we won."

"We?"

"I'm your support system. Without a coach, a competitor is nothing."

"Mm-hmm."

Weirdly, Sarissa is right. People who had previously ignored us approach to congratulate me, and Sarissa jokes with them, compliments them, and makes contacts left and right.

I grin as she's suddenly deep in conversation with a Braxian male.

"Oh, your sister is a metalsmith? We've got someone working on our thruster, but if it doesn't work out, maybe she could help us."

I keep quiet as the vendor hands me my prize, a smile on her face. "I will need to make this more difficult for you next time, hmm?"

I grin, glancing at Sarissa, who is currently elbowing a guy so large he's practically a giant. She jokingly challenges him to a wrestling match, and he throws his head back, his laugh booming over the crowd.

It's then I see the commander, standing on the outskirts of the crowd, staring at my cousin, his face blank. He turns his attention to me, and I give him a tiny wave.

Why is he following us?

The crowd begins to thin as Sarissa sidles up to me. "That guy said his sister is dating a Zinta," she murmurs as we wander away from the kradi. "I wonder how much the Zinta talks about their plans."

I raise one eyebrow. "And you say you're not a spy."

She simply smiles.

I nod toward the spot where the commander was standing. "Korzyn followed us. I saw him a few minutes ago, although he disappeared when you finished charming the crowd."

Her smile drops. "That mothertrucker. He's cruising for a bruising, he is."

We head toward the woman who ordered the replacement part for our thruster. She shakes her head at us as we arrive, and I sigh. It was too much to expect that her contact could have arrived already. All we can do is keep checking in and hope he makes his way to this part of the galaxy soon.

After a night with such little sleep, I'm tired, so I persuade Sarissa to come back to the castle with me. She gives in surprisingly easily, and I eye her as we get back in the hydro.

"I would've thought you'd want to stay for longer."

"I do, but not if that grim-faced commander is spying on us. Next time, we'll lose him first."

"Uh-huh."

She tilts her head, gesturing behind us, where the guards Arix assigned us are in their own hydro. "Those guys are bad enough, and you know they're reporting to Korzyn anyway. So that makes me wonder just why Korzyn is paranoid enough to want to follow us himself. And when I start wondering things like that, I have what some would call a desperate need to get answers. Let's see how the commander feels when the shoe is on *my* foot."

I sigh. "This is definitely going to bite us in the ass," I mumble.

We settle in for the ride, and I watch the Braxians going about their day as we travel down the river. A flower vendor sells her wares on a corner, handing a small blue flower to an old man, who grins at her as he passes by. A noblewoman stalks down the street, dressed to the nines and flanked by guards. Three boys race each other through an alley, their mother calling after them.

I'm so entranced that Sarissa has to nudge me when we arrive, gesturing for me to get out of the hydro.

"I'm going to go explore," she says.

"Have fun. I'm going to take a nap."

But I don't head straight up to my rooms. Instead, I make my way to the throne room and peek in the door. The guards are silent behind me, and I attempt to ignore them, pretending I'm not inexplicably drawn to their king like a moth to a flame.

I must be watching some kind of meeting because there are a group of people standing in front of the throne, and Arix's face is serious as he listens to them.

He glances up, and his eyes instantly find mine, the look in them predatory. The hair on the back of my neck rises, my instincts telling me I'm being hunted. Heads begin to turn, his subjects likely wondering what he's looking at, and I back away, almost ramming into a guard who introduced himself earlier as Zion.

"How do I get back to my rooms?" I ask him, and he turns to lead me toward them.

"Wait."

I freeze as Arix's low voice caresses my ears. It feels as if he has a hand wrapped around my throat and he's squeezing—not hard enough to kill, but enough to let me know in no uncertain terms that he's in charge.

It pisses me off.

I school my face into boredom and turn, lifting one eyebrow.

He's so beautiful that a bolt of resentment hits me in the chest. He seems to know it, because he gives me a savage smile.

"Leave," he orders, and the guards file out of the room.

"That was rude. Why *are* you having me escorted from place to place like a prisoner anyway?"

"Partly for your own protection. Partly because my commander believes you and your cousin are a threat."

I snort at that. What kind of threat could we possibly be to these huge men with their swords and their scowls?

"What did you do today?"

I shift on my feet. "You want to chat? Here?"

"No. I want to eat your cunt for my midday meal, but since that doesn't seem to be on the table, I decided I would get to know you until you throw away whatever ridiculous excuses are preventing you from tumbling me."

Heat spreads up my body, traveling from my toes to the top of my head. I have an instant vision of me sitting on his desk in front of him, my legs spread as he grins up at me, that exact hungry look in his eyes.

He smiles as if reading my mind. "What exactly are you thinking about now, lovely?" he asks as he prowls closer.

I clear my throat. "Nothing." Truthfully, the more time I spend around this guy, and the more the air crackles between us, the more I wonder if I shouldn't just live in the moment and take what he's offering.

From the triumphant look on Arix's face, he's reading that thought too. Am I that transparent? I force my face to go blank, and this seems to amuse him even more.

"Why the hesitation, Vivian? Are you untried?"

I frown at that. Un— "No!" While I may not be all that experienced, my cherry has indeed been popped. There's no inconvenient skin tag waiting to get in the way of Arix's—

No, girl, don't go there.

His smile widens. "Then what is the problem?"

What *is* the problem?

"I don't want to get pregnant."

The words are out of my mouth before I can stop them, and he frowns. This isn't my only objection, of course, but now that I've said it, flying through space with a bun in my oven *would* definitely be a bummer.

"There are ways around that," Arix murmurs, stepping even closer. I glance around us, but we're still alone, and I'm suddenly pressed up against the cool black stone of the wall, the king leaning into my personal space like he owns it.

I clear my throat, hoping he can't see exactly how much his nearness affects me. "What do you mean?"

"The petals of a specific flower will prevent any inconvenient problems."

Inconvenient problems? Maybe for him. For me, it would be a life-changing catastrophe.

"I will keep you safe, lovely. You have only to trust me."

I nibble on my lip, and his eyes drop. And then his mouth is on mine, his hand buried in my hair as he thrusts his tongue between my lips. I groan as he hardens against my stomach, and I suddenly need the thick length of him to be much, much lower.

The kiss is over in moments, and I stare at him, panting. He looks unaffected, his face blank, but his eyes are burning and the thick bulge in his pants shows just how affected he is.

I feel...powerful to be able to make this arrogant king want me so desperately.

"Just a preview," he smiles, but his eyes are still hungry. "You'll have to agree to my terms for what you really need."

He swipes his tongue along his teeth and then turns, stalking away, and I watch him go. *What exactly are his terms?*

CHAPTER FOUR

A rix

I'm sneaking back from the dock, the hood of my cloak hiding my face when I smell it.

Smoke.

It gets thicker in the air the closer I am to the castle, and I break into a run.

There's no logical reason for the heavy ball of dread in my stomach, but I know with absolute certainty that something is very wrong.

I jolt awake, cursing. The dreams have plagued me since I lost my parents, but the more attacks there are on my guards, the more frequent the dreams.

I'm running out of time.

I need something to distract me just enough that I can get through the nights but not enough to risk my goals.

Someone to distract me.

Enough is enough. I want the lovely human female, and she wants me. The only barrier is her stubbornness.

I get up, thanking the servant who arrives with the first meal of the day. He offers to help me dress, and I wave him away—the same dance we do each morning.

I'm sitting on my balcony, eating and contemplating my schedule for the day, when Korzyn arrives.

"I noticed you were nowhere to be found yesterday morning," I remark, and he growls and mutters something under his breath as he takes the chair next to me. He's frowning, his eyes distant, and I tilt my head as I study him.

It's not often that someone distracts him.

"I followed the human females to the marketplace."

"I could have sworn I assigned several of my most trustworthy guards to that exact task."

He scowls at me. "I wanted to handle it myself."

"Mm-hmm. And did you see them getting up to all kinds of nefarious plots? Perhaps they were gathering an army to take over my kingdom?"

His scowl deepens. "You're in a good mood."

I...am. And I have a sneaking suspicion it has something to do with the lush mouth I felt briefly under mine yesterday. It's only a matter of time before I have more than Vivian's mouth beneath me, and for the first time in years, a female has given me the thrill of the hunt.

"So tell me, what did the females do that warranted the commander of my forces watching them so closely, even while they were guarded the entire time?"

Korzyn raises one eyebrow. "Do you truly think your enemies won't use any weaknesses they can find? One look at your face when that female is in the room, and it's obvious she is a crack where you can least afford to have any weaknesses. They will approach her, likely offering her anything she wants in exchange for her help when they finally decide to move on you."

I nod, my good mood vanishing. "I'm expecting as much."

Korzyn's eyes widen minutely, the most surprise he will allow on his face. "You're using her as bait."

"Very pretty bait, but bait just the same. Bait that won't be taken if you're so close to Vivian that our enemies can't approach her."

He frowns but considers my words. "And the other female?"

I wave my hand dismissively. "Stay as close to her as you like if you truly believe she is a threat. I yield to your paranoia."

"Paranoia saves lives. It has saved your life more than once."

I match his frown. "Indeed."

* * *

Vivian

I barge into Sarissa's rooms, not at all surprised to find that she's also still in her nightclothes. After another night of tossing and turning, I gave up on sleep, sneaking out of my rooms when I heard Cauri arrive.

I pad through her sitting room but hesitate as my eyes are drawn to English writing on a pile of papers sitting on her table.

I don't want to pry, but I lean over anyway. Sarissa isn't exactly being herself lately.

The top page is a list of everything she knows about the

Grivath, including their planet, their war against the Arcav, and their alliances. My hands itch to read the rest, but I force myself to back away. She'll talk to me about it when she's ready.

Sarissa looks like she had as much sleep as I did, and she frowns at me as I walk into her bedroom.

"What happened to you yesterday? I looked for you in your rooms, but the guard on the door said you were near the throne room."

I have a sudden vision of the bulge in Arix's pants, and my body heats.

A slow grin spreads over her face. "Something happened. Gimme."

"Arix kissed me."

"Oooh. Was it good?"

I blush as I get a sudden flashback.

His lips, hard on mine. His tongue, pressing into my mouth like he owns it. The heat of him against me, so close to where I want him.

Sarissa's grin widens. "Whoa. It was that good, huh?"

I fan my face with one hand. "The man has moves, that's for sure."

The strange thing is, while he was laying on the charm before he kissed me, after he pulled away, there was no hiding the fact he was just as affected as I was.

Sarissa nudges me with her foot. "So the king wants to bone you. Are you going to do it?"

"Maybe. I've never had this kind of chemistry with anyone, you know?"

"Oh, I know." Her tone is wry, and I groan. Sarissa knows all about my lack of experience. She's one of the few people who I could trust with the gory details of how my ex-boyfriend Mike came before he even got inside my vagina.

And then again when my crush Joe literally lasted for ten seconds the first time I had sex. It's mortifying.

"He said it would be no-strings," I say.

She grins. "My favorite kind of relationship. Well, if you're up for it, I think you should do it. Your poor coochie is probably crying out for some D."

I groan again. "I hate you."

Sarissa laughs, and I pick up the pillow by my side.

Then I slam it into her face.

She narrows her eyes at me. "Oh, this is war."

I shriek, taking the pillow and running into her sitting room as she sprints after me. My cousin is still a bully, and I'm still poking the bear, only to end up eaten when the bear wakes up.

I dodge around the couch, but she swings her pillow, hitting me in the side of the head, and I stumble.

"Bitch."

I'm out of breath—from both the laughing and the running—and Sarissa giggles as I aim my pillow and miss.

I laugh harder as she steps back, her heel catching the edge of her long nightgown. She stumbles, almost falling on her ass. None of the other women would recognize my cousin right now, that's for sure. She bares her teeth at me, swinging her pillow again, but I'm ready for it—thanks to Nevada's insistence that I train with the other women during their morning classes.

I duck, swinging my pillow at the same time and slamming it into her stomach.

Sarissa howls, her eyes lighting up with vengeance, and I swallow as she steps toward me. Uh-oh. I turn to run again, freezing as I come face-to-face with Arix and Korzyn.

They're standing in the doorway staring at us, their eyes

wide. Behind them, Cauri has her hands on her hips, her face twisted in disapproval.

Oh shit.

Sarissa stumbles into me, and we both reach for each other, barely managing to keep on our feet. We must look like a couple of clowns, and Arix stares at us, the corner of his mouth twitching. Korzyn's gaze is glued to my cousin, who looks wild, her hair tumbling around her shoulders, face flushed, aqua eyes glowing.

She clears her throat, pushing her hair off her face, and the smile disappears. I'm sad to see it go. My cousin doesn't smile enough anymore.

"Good morning, gentlemen."

"Don't let us stop you," Arix says, gesturing for us to continue, and I squirm in embarrassment. His eyes are lit with amusement, and I shrug. If he didn't want us to act like children, he shouldn't have given us beds stacked with approximately nine hundred pillows.

Arix's brow raises at our awkward silence, the corner of his mouth twitching.

"I was wondering if you'd like to join us for the midday meal," he says. "I try to eat with my advisers and some of my guards occasionally. It'll be a good opportunity for you to meet them, since you'll be staying here until you can fix your ship. It's close to the river with a view I think you'll both like."

There's no trace of the man who dropped the "c-bomb" yesterday while staring at me like I was the sun and he was freezing to death. I don't know what this new tactic is, but whatever his true reasons are for inviting us here, his generosity is allowing us to have a real chance of getting off this planet.

I glance at Sarissa. I'm down if she is. She nods, and I

smile at Arix, pulling my robe tighter around myself. "That sounds great."

The guys leave, and I groan as Cauri glares at me, pointing her finger toward my room. Great, now I've pissed off my maid. Given that she likes to show her displeasure when she does my hair, I'll be surprised if I have any left after this.

Sarissa snorts, Hesa—her own maid—waiting quietly, her face amused, behind Cauri.

"Good luck with *that*," Sarissa murmurs, and I scowl at her.

"Just you wait. My revenge will be swift and sweet."

"Uh-huh. Keep telling yourself that, V."

Cauri lectures me the entire time she's helping me get ready. I manage to tune out most of it until she decides my hair simply must go in a complicated updo if I'm having a meal with the king. The sharp tug of her brush down my hair reminds me of my mother getting me ready for pageants as a kid, and I'm so tense I'm about to put my foot down and tell her to leave when she pushes one last pin in my hair and steps back.

"There. Now you look like a lovely female and not a romping child," she says.

I roll my eyes. "We were having fun."

Cauri frowns as if the concept is completely foreign to her, and I sigh, getting to my feet.

I'm wearing a long forest-green dress. The material itself has some kind of soft-gold sheen to it, and it shimmers in the light. My hair has been brushed, curled, and braided into submission, and my scalp aches. I'll last approximately half an hour with this tension on my scalp before I take it down. I'm not planning to end up in bed with a migraine today.

My stomach flutters at the thought of being in bed for an entirely different reason, and I can't help but think of the intrigued look in Arix's eyes when he stared at me in Sarissa's room.

The king is arrogant, suggestive, and charming. But beneath all that, I occasionally get glimpses of a man I'd like to know better.

Cauri nudges me, dragging me from my daydream.

"What are you waiting for, silly girl? Don't be late!"

I sigh. "Thank you for helping me get ready."

She harrumphs, turning away, but I catch the surprise on her face. Do people not usually thank her for her work?

Sarissa meets me outside my door, and I glower at her. "How come you get a ponytail and I get this?"

She attempts to hide a smirk as she stares at my complicated updo. "Because I'm not scared of my maid, that's why."

I narrow my eyes. "I'm not scared of her."

Cauri opens my door and glares at us, and I jump.

"Go!"

I jolt into motion, ignoring Sarissa's low laugh.

"Not scared, huh?"

"Shut up."

CHAPTER FIVE

V ivian

The guards escort us close to the dock behind the castle, but we don't get into a hydro. Instead, we cross a long bridge over the river, walking down a stone path for a few minutes before it opens up to a large clearing.

To the left, the river flows, hydros full of people traveling up and down the water, many of them craning their heads to get a glimpse of the king. To the right, a large group of tables and chairs has been set up, and servants are busy placing huge dishes laden with food on the tables.

Arix sits at the head of the longest table, talking to a few men who are nodding in agreement with whatever he's saying.

"Ah, here they are," he says as we approach, still surrounded by our guards. "Vivian, you remember Bevix?"

Bevix is the adviser who interrupted the first time Arix was propositioning me. The one Arix was determined wouldn't see me in my "nightclothes." Honestly, the night-clothes here cover more than the clothes I would wear to the mall on Earth, but from the frown on Arix's face, he's likely remembering that little interaction. And he's still not happy about it.

"Nice to see you again," I murmur to Bevix, ignoring Arix's warning look. Bevix introduces himself to Sarissa, who nods her hello, and then Arix gestures to the older man on his left.

"This is Tridi. My father's brother."

Tridi smiles at me, his face puzzled as he runs his eyes over Sarissa and me. He's Arix's uncle, then, but from the cold look on Arix's face, there's no love lost between them.

I find myself intrigued by Arix's life here. For some reason, I'm almost desperate to know all about his inner circle. I want to know who he trusts and why, who he considers family, and the problems keeping him up at night.

It's just because he's a king. Sure, Rakiz and Dexar are kings of their tribes, but Arix obviously rules over a much larger territory and many more people. It's natural for me to want to learn everything I can about a king on an alien planet.

Mm-hmm. It's his history you have a fascination with. Not his body. Keep telling yourself that.

"This is Rachiv," he says, nodding toward the guy sitting next to Tridi. "He is also one of my most trusted advisers."

Rachiv doesn't look at all impressed with us. In fact, he's looking at me the way I used to look at the three-day-old sandwich I'd occasionally find in my purse.

I see you, I tell him with my eyes, and he waits until Arix begins introducing us to someone else before he sneers back at me.

Dickhead.

Arix gestures to a couple of servants, who begin pulling out chairs for us to sit in. I blink, hesitating until Sarissa plunks her butt in her seat and raises her eyebrow at me. I kind of assumed we would be sitting at one of the smaller tables surrounding this one, perhaps closer to the edge of the forest or on the other side—near the river. I hadn't imagined we'd be sitting at the "royal table," and from the look on Rachiv's face, he feels the same way.

Korzyn appears, leaning down to murmur in Arix's ear. Arix shakes his head, gesturing to the empty seat next to Sarissa, and Korzyn's scowl is so deep I almost laugh.

"So," Bevix says, once we're seated and the servants fill our cups. "What is it that you do on your planet? I must admit I'm fascinated at the way you ended up on Agron."

I smile at him, and he nods at me. He can obviously feel the tension as well as I can, and he's attempting to make us feel welcome.

Arix's midnight eyes find mine, and he raises one dark eyebrow. "Yes," he says. "The human females are indeed *intriguing.*"

I stare at him, willing myself not to blush. Thankfully, this time, my cheeks don't heat. Maybe I'm getting better at this.

Bevix glances between me and Sarissa, obviously waiting for an answer.

"I'd tell you, but then I'd have to kill you," Sarissa says sweetly, and the entire table freezes.

Good move, Sarissa. I grind my teeth, shooting her a look, and she sends me a wicked grin.

Next to her, Korzyn is practically vibrating with tension.

I clear my throat, channeling my mother with an airy laugh. "That's an Earth joke," I explain with a wave of my hand.

"I don't find it amusing," Korzyn says.

"You wouldn't," Sarissa mutters, and I kick her beneath the table.

She sighs. "I work for our country's government. I'm one of thousands of people who help protect our country from foreign threats."

Korzyn is studying her like she's a bug he'd quite enjoy dissecting.

She sends him a cool look and then smiles at the table at large, and several of Arix's advisers can't help but smile back. It's not often that Sarissa turns on the charm, but when she does, it's like standing under the heat of the sun. You can't help but bask in the warmth.

At least that's how one of her ex-boyfriends described her to me when I ran into him at a bar three months after they broke up.

"It's pretty boring, really. Vivian has a much more exciting job. Why don't you tell them about it, V?"

I grind my teeth at that.

"Wow, I'm hungry," I say. "This is a beautiful setting, by the way. Thanks for inviting us."

Arix says nothing, his eyes hot on my face.

"And what is your '*job*,' then?" he murmurs.

"I model."

"Model." He tastes the word, saying it in English because there's obviously no Braxian equivalent.

The entire table seems to be staring at me, even people situated down at the other end, who are craning their heads.

I get it, of course. Korzyn likely has questions about Sarissa's job that she can't explain without sounding exactly like what he thinks she is.

A spy.

Unfortunately, that means she has to throw me under

the bus.

Thanks, Rissa. Why don't you back that bus over me while you're at it?

"On Earth, brands hire me to wear their designs. I'm photographed in their clothes so that others can see those clothes and hopefully decide to buy them."

It takes an eternity to explain what a photograph is, and a couple of Arix's advisers seem to think we're playing with them, while Rachiv murmurs that it sounds like sorcery.

The first course has been taken away by the time they understand how cameras work.

Arix's eyes are now burning into mine. "And people keep these...pictures of you?"

"Ummm, I don't know if they keep them," I hedge, and Sarissa snorts.

"Remember that one stalker you had a few years ago? He sent threatening notes, and all the letters had been cut out of the newspaper." She laughs. "So old school." She grins at Arix. "The police eventually got enough for a search warrant, and the psycho had an honest-to-God shrine set up for my baby cousin. He had every photo ever taken of her, I swear."

That's it. I kick Sarissa under the table again. "What is your deal?" I hiss at her while Arix scowls at both of us, clearly perturbed by her stalker story.

"Just laying the groundwork, V."

With that nonanswer, she digs into her stew with relish.

The table turns to small talk, the advisers telling funny stories, all attempting to outdo one another for the king's amusement. It's clear they appreciate this time with him, and he listens to them, occasionally commenting or laughing at a joke.

Tiny, sweet pastries have been placed in front of us, and

they're almost demolished when Arix's dark eyes find mine again.

"Vivian," he purrs. "Will you take a walk with me?"

I blush as all attention is suddenly on me, fighting the urge to throw the last bite of my pastry at him. His eyes spark as if he's reading my mind.

"Sure," I mutter gracelessly, and his smile widens. He gets to his feet, striding around the table and offering me his arm as I rise from my own seat.

I take it, attempting to ignore the silence that has descended. From the surprised look on Tridi's face, whatever Arix is up to is out of the ordinary. Bevix winks at me, and Arix places his hand over mine, leading me away from the table.

He shakes his head at his guards as they attempt to follow us, and they stop in their tracks.

"Where are we going?" I ask.

"It's a surprise."

We walk in companionable silence for a while, heading further away from the river, the sun behind us. The sounds of people talking fade away, and soon there are only the chirp of birds and the rustle of animals foraging for food.

"It's so peaceful here."

Arix nods. He directs me between two trees, and we leave the forest path. He helps me climb over a fallen tree, then lifts me over a few large rocks.

We walk up a hill, and I'm slightly breathless when we finally get to the top.

"Wow."

We're in some kind of garden. Only, it's nothing like the beautiful yet ruthlessly manicured gardens surrounding the castle. This is undomesticated and unkept, a free-for-all of flowers and plants.

Wildflowers bloom throughout, with little thought given to color selection or plant type. The bright colors clash in places, but the garden is all the more charming for its chaos.

From here, we have a view of the river, but anyone sitting in a hydro would have to squint to see us, hidden as we are through the trees.

It's natural, disorderly, and untamed. I love it.

"What is this place?"

Arix gestures to a wooden bench on one side, surrounded by huge yellow flowers shaped similar to poppies on earth.

I take a seat, and he sits next to me, throwing one hand over the back of the bench. He instantly looks more relaxed than I've seen him since I met him.

"This was my mother's place. She loved gardening and would often attempt to help the gardeners when they were working around the castle. But people gossiped. They said it was unseemly for the queen to be working like a servant.

"She was brokenhearted, but my father brought her here. He said he'd discovered it during one of his walks and it was waiting for her special touch. My mother didn't make many changes—most of these flowers were already growing in the area, and she added a few she felt would do well here. But she loved this place. We'd sit right here when I was a child, and she would make me tell her all my problems."

He smiles, and my heart thumps harder in my chest. Arix is beautiful, and every smirk and wicked grin he sends my way gives me butterflies. But the simple, sad smile, the fondness in his eyes when he speaks of his mom...

This is the real Arix.

"She sounds like an amazing mom." I hope the jealousy I feel at the thought of growing up with a mom like her isn't evident in my voice.

Arix removes his arm from across the top of the bench and throws it around my shoulders. "She was."

"Do you mind if I ask what happened to your parents?"

"They were murdered."

My mouth drops open. I expected some kind of accident. For some reason, foul play hadn't crossed my mind.

I glance at him, and he pulls me closer. He's not looking at me, and I reach out, placing my hand on his knee.

He turns his head, gazing down at me. "A little higher, beauty."

I scowl at him, removing my hand. "I was being supportive."

Surprise flashes across his face, as if he's not used to anyone offering him comfort. The thought makes me sad for him, and I don't protest when he drags me closer, using his other hand to grab my wrist and pressing his lips to my palm.

"Do you know who killed them?"

He shakes his head. "To this day, I am working to discover who could have done such a thing. Unfortunately, a court as large as my parents' had multiple suspects. I have my own suspicions, but my father would expect me to only act once I have proof."

His lips twist at that, and my throat tightens. I'm guessing he'd like to round up all his suspects and torture the information out of them. But he's still attempting to honor his dad.

I shiver as he strokes the sensitive skin along my wrist, and he smiles. The bastard knows exactly what he does to me.

He studies my face. "Why do you want to go back to your planet so badly?"

I shrug. "It's home."

He leans down and picks a flower before handing it to me, and I smile, inhaling the light fragrance.

"Earth isn't perfect, that's for sure. In a lot of ways, it's a goddamned shitshow. It's full of wars and hunger and death. With a big ol' helping of inequality and sadness. Just when you think you're winning the game, the rules change and you're suddenly losing."

Arix tilts his head, and I smile.

"But it's beautiful too, with sights that make you pinch yourself they're so incredible. There's hope around every corner. People who care about each other. People who sacrifice for others. But most importantly, it's ours."

He studies my face for a long moment and then nods. "I understand. My kingdom has its faults, and while I try to improve it every day, it will always be a work in progress. But if someone were to take it from me, I would not rest until I had taken it back. My father would expect nothing less."

"I guess we have more in common than I thought."

He grins, his eyes sharpening on my face. Then he lowers his head, giving me plenty of time to stop him, but I don't, allowing him to cover my mouth with his.

His lips are firm and hot, and he uses the arm around my shoulders to hold me in place as he plunders my mouth. My thighs tense, and I gasp as my body goes languid and soft against him.

He slowly pulls away, and my heart stutters at the lust written all over his face.

"Come to my rooms after dinner," he murmurs. "And let me show you how much more we have in common."

I open my mouth, but we both turn at the sound of someone clomping through the bushes.

"They went in this direction," a low voice says, and Arix tenses, immediately pulling me to my feet and striding toward the intruder. He's practically dragging me at this point, but I get it.

This is his sanctuary, and he sure doesn't want others to know about it.

It's Tridi who's striding along the forest path, two guards in tow. He looks surprised when we appear from within the forest, and I clear my throat.

"I saw the cutest furry animal and insisted we get closer," I laugh, batting my lashes for good measure. "His Majesty was kind enough to help me."

Tridi nods, his brow creasing, but he seems to accept that explanation. Arix takes my hand and squeezes it, the gesture not missed by Tridi's keen eyes.

"I was hoping to talk to you," Tridi says, and Arix nods.

"I'll be right there."

Tridi glances between us, raising his eyebrows. Then he nods, turning back toward the clearing where we had lunch, chatting to his guards as he leaves. Unlike mine and Sarissa's guards, his are obviously for *his* protection, while ours seem to have been put in place to protect everyone else from whatever threat we apparently present.

Arix squeezes my hand again, and I jump, realizing I've been frowning after Tridi. His eyes are serious, and he leans close, murmuring in my ear.

"You are never to be alone with him," he says, and my mouth drops open.

"What? Why?"

"Promise me."

I search his face, and from his lowered brows and the sharp jut of his chin, it's obvious this is important to him.

"I promise."

"Good." He turns and strides away.

CHAPTER SIX

V ivian

I walk back with Sarissa, our guards trailing at a distance. Neither of us wants to go back to our rooms just yet, so we head toward the gardens. The neat rows of flowers and shorter grass make these gardens lovely to walk through, but they don't come close to matching Arix's mom's wild garden, hidden from view all these years.

Sarissa is quiet, and I nudge her with my elbow. "What's up?"

She sighs. "Nothing. I just feel bad for leaving the other women. Clara was pissed when I said I'd go with you. She told me leaders don't get to just quit when the going is tough. She said we may have found help, but part of leadership was providing emotional support and stability."

I scowl at that. "You're of more help here, looking for a way off this planet, than you are being a shoulder to cry on back at camp."

"I'm worried I made the wrong choice."

"Well, I'm worried about you."

Her eyes widen slightly. "What do you mean?"

"I saw your notes on the Grivath."

She shrugs. "I want revenge. That's no secret."

"What if we can't get off this planet?"

"Oh, we're getting off this planet. I don't care who I have to kill to make it happen."

I glance around us, but the guards are giving us more privacy than usual, chatting amongst themselves.

"This doesn't sound like you, Rissa."

Are those tears sparkling in her aqua eyes? I can count on one hand the number of times I've seen my cousin cry.

"You don't understand, V. When we were on that ship...I thought we were going to die. We all did. And then Kelly really did die. Some of those women...a few of them are still teenagers. They're so young, and they were losing their minds. I promised them we'd get out of there. I know I shouldn't have made any promises, but I swore we'd make the Grivath pay for what they did. And now we have a chance to do exactly that."

I sigh. I get it now. "And you always keep your promises."

She nods, her face hard, all signs of tears gone. "That's right."

I know not to say it, but I say it anyway.

"You can't let what happened impact your entire life. It's not your fault, Rissa. You couldn't have saved her."

She immediately shuts down, her eyes flashing warningly at me. "I'm not talking about this."

"Sarissa..."

"Not. Talking. About. It."

"Fine!" I throw up my hands. "God, you're stubborn."

"Aw, thanks, V. That means a lot coming from you."

I growl, and she laughs, brushing a stray tear off her face. "Soooo what did you and Mr. Tall, Dark, and Royal talk about?"

"Not much. His parents were murdered. Did you know that?"

She nods. "I learned that on our first day here. I thought you knew. According to most people, the king and queen were well liked, and known as fair rulers with a penchant for helping the poor. They had some policies that were unpopular amongst the wealthier people here—similar to tax increases on Earth. But they had no true enemies."

"So whoever killed them was likely to be someone who wanted their throne."

"Yeah. I thought it might be Arix at first. After all, he was supposed to be in the royal quarters with them. He'd snuck out that night. But he was just a kid, really, and everyone says he adored—and was adored by—his parents. Plus, he attempted to get into the royal quarters to save them while it was burning."

Sarissa's face twists, and my heart does the same.

"Rissa..."

"I'm okay. Anyway, the uncle is obviously suspect numero uno. After all, if Arix dies, he's the one most likely to take the throne. But some say he wouldn't be able to keep it—he hasn't been working on his alliances enough over the years. After him, there are a bunch of advisers who would at least rule temporarily, and get this: the commander could be in the running for the throne too."

I tilt my head. "You think the commander could've done it?"

She shrugs. "Anyone is a suspect."

"Arix told me not to be alone with his uncle today."

"Probably a good idea to not be alone with any of these

guys. Except maybe Arix if you're planning to let him get under your dress." She winks at me. "So are you?"

I blow out a breath. "I've been working on a pros and cons list."

She laughs. "Of course you have. Let's hear it."

"Okay. Pro: He makes me feel...good. He doesn't see me as just a dumb model, although I guess that's because he doesn't really know what a model is. Thanks for that little peek into my life at lunch, by the way."

"You're welcome."

"Con: He's *way* more experienced than me."

"Girl, that's a pro. Why would you want to be with someone who *you* have to tell what to do in bed?" She wrinkles her nose. "Not fun."

"Hmm. Okay, so you may have a point there."

"Of course I do. Go on, give me the rest of it."

I lean over and smell a bright-red flower, stroking one finger over the soft petals.

"Pro: It would be a chance for me to have some *fun* on Agron, you know? Everyone else has been banging all over the place, and I'm still practically a virgin. It's embarrassing."

Sarissa bursts out laughing. "Agreed. And con?"

I glance at the guards behind us. "It feels weird to consider boning someone who has guards following us around."

She snorts. "I can guarantee the guards were at the commander's insistence. From what I've learned about *him*, Korzyn is about as trusting as a murder cop three days from retirement. Don't worry about him though. I'm going to find out what makes him tick. And then I'm going to kill it."

I gape at her, and we both jump as one of the guards clears his throat.

We both whirl. "You guys are surprisingly quiet for such huge men," I mutter, and Zion grins at me while the other guard stays blank-faced. Sarissa narrows her eyes at both guards.

"Snitches get stitches," she advises them, and I sigh. They are definitely going to tell the commander that we were up to no good. As if the guy needs any further excuse to glower at us.

We turn and continue walking, this time glancing frequently over our shoulders to check just how close the guards are.

"Okay, then. Con?" Sarissa asks, her voice low.

"I just don't know if I'm the fling type. Other than a glimpse of sadness when he talked about his mom, I've never seen any real feelings from Arix."

"That's a good thing. You don't *want* feelings from a fling. Look, this is the best-case scenario for an elongated one-night stand. No awkward phone calls, no bumping into him when you're out with friends—or worse, a new guy—and certainly no pondering whether to have another fling in the future. You'll get it out of your system and then leave. It's perfect."

I narrow my eyes at her. "You seem way too invested in this."

She sighs. "You've been sad, V. And I get it. It's hard seeing everyone else settling down with their Braxians. Now you'll get a little slice of that, but you'll still be able to get on that ship and kick some Grivath ass. It's a win-win."

"You realize absolutely none of that was about Arix himself, right?"

She shrugs. "He's just a man. A very good-looking man, but a man all the same. And we don't catch feelings." She smiles. "We catch spaceships."

I think about her words while I walk back to the castle. Before I know it, I'm standing outside Arix's rooms, after convincing Zion to take me to them. I knock, but he doesn't answer, so I shrug, scampering back to my room where I can pretend nothing happened.

I pace for a while, still adding to my pros and cons list. I'm being ridiculous, I know... But if I trust my traitorous body to make the decision...

I'll be climbing all over him.

I turn at a knock on the door, my stomach fluttering as it opens. Arix stands there, his eyes on mine as if he can see through them and read all my inner thoughts.

"Korzyn said you were looking for me," he says.

I frown. "I never told him that."

He gives me a look, and I roll my eyes. Our guards told Korzyn, who told Arix. Got it.

"I've been thinking," I say, and Arix studies my face. Whatever he sees must please him, because he smiles and closes the door.

"And?"

He prowls toward me, and I swallow, suddenly nervous.

"And...I want to..."

"Yes?"

He's enjoying this far too much, his eyes lit with amusement.

I scowl at him. "Forget it."

He laughs. "You're a prickly female. Tell me what you want, Vivian, and I will give it to you."

The words are so suggestive that I almost expect him to accompany the last part of his sentence with a hip thrust.

"You're right, okay? I haven't had sex in a while, and I guess I do need it."

His face turns serious. "It's not *tumbling* you need. It's tumbling with *me*. Say it."

I narrow my eyes at him. "You have a lot of demands for a guy who wants to get laid."

He laughs, but his eyes are intent as he steps even closer. He's so close that the scent of him teases my nostrils, making me want to close my eyes and breathe him in.

"I want you." I blush as soon as I say it, and his face hardens.

"Finally."

He buries his hand in my hair, taking my mouth. I groan against him, but then he's spinning me around, directing me toward my bed.

"Wait. We're doing this now?"

His laugh is low and rough. "You think I'm waiting after you finally told me you want me? No. If you want me to stop, tell me now, and I'll leave. If you don't, I'll make you feel more pleasure than you've ever felt before."

His voice is low in my ear as he stands behind me, his arm wrapped around my waist as he pushes my hair aside. He kisses along the back of my neck, and I shudder as warmth blossoms in my stomach.

"Choose, Vivian."

Something about the way he says my name makes me giddy.

"Yes."

The word is barely out before he's hauling me back toward my bed again. He begins undoing my dress, kissing every inch of my bare skin as it's revealed, and I sigh, squirming against him.

My dress drops to the floor, and I'm suddenly in nothing except the thin stockings Cauri insisted I wear. I reach back, wanting him to be just as naked as I am. But his hands are on my body, pushing and pulling until I'm where he wants me—on all fours. I blush as I glance over my shoulder, finding him standing behind me, still as stone.

His eyes are burning as he stares at my pussy and ass. "No underwear for you, then?"

I smile. "They're too confining."

Something like pain crosses his face. "Now every time I look at you, I'll know you're naked under those dresses."

I grin, and it's probably smug, because his eyes heat further.

"You enjoy making me lose focus?"

My grin widens. He drives me out of my mind. Why shouldn't I do the same to him?

"Filthy female," he murmurs, his eyes glinting with lust.

I blush harder, and I almost move, hopelessly embarrassed.

"Don't," he says.

I bury my face in the blanket as he positions himself behind me, his mouth finding me as he licks and plays, flicking my clit as he inserts two fingers into me. I groan into the blanket, and then his hand is in my hair, encouraging me to lift my head.

"I want to hear you."

That somehow drives me higher, and he rewards my moans with long strokes of his tongue.

My orgasm unfurls from my center, shimmering through my body until I collapse, gasping.

Arix leans over and nibbles along my neck while I rub myself against him, attempting to align myself with the huge cock I glimpsed a few minutes ago. I'm not sure exactly how he plans to fit that thing in my vagina, but I'm up for the challenge.

Arix growls and hauls me back up to my hands and

knees, plunging into me without warning. My hands reach out, scrabbling at the blanket as I clamp down around him, immediately on edge again.

He circles his hips, hitting all the spots inside me that make me moan, and then he's clutching my hips in his huge hands, holding me still as he slams inside me. He's impossibly big in this position, and I open my mouth, about to protest, but he slips his hand down to my clit and all thought leaves my brain.

He lets out a growl as I tighten around him, and then he's the one losing that control he's so fond of. He pulls me up onto my knees, one hand on my breast, the other on my clit, as he grinds himself into me. He plays with my nipple and then moves that hand up, circling my throat, his touch possessive.

"Mine," he growls, and the word throws me over, making me shudder in his arms as pleasure rips through every inch of my body. He thrusts twice more and then stills, breathing heavily as he pulls me even closer.

I don't know whether to chide him for his arrogance or high-five him for being right.

He *did* give me more pleasure than I ever felt before. We're both still gasping as he pulls out of me, and I feel immediately empty as he moves away.

He runs one hand along my spine with a hum, and then he disappears for a moment before reappearing with a damp cloth, which he presses between my legs while I attempt not to blush. From his low laugh, he can tell just how embarrassed I am.

"Shit. We didn't use a condom."

His face is blank as I roll over, and he's still gloriously naked, hardening once more as his gaze finds my breasts and seems to get stuck there. He plucks at my nipple, and I groan.

His eyes light, and I raise my hand, covering his mouth as he leans down.

"Protection. No babies, remember?"

Understanding flashes across his face, and he pulls my hand away. "I will have a tonic sent to you tonight with dinner. It's made with the petals of a flower with contraceptive properties. If you take it each day, you will not conceive."

I sigh. I barely know Arix, but for some reason, I trust him with this. Something tells me he'd be as panicked about a surprise baby as I would be.

I stroke my hands over his shoulders, fascinated by the green-and-blue scales that gleam in the light.

He's waiting for me to answer, and I nod, waving a hand the way I've seen him do when he's sitting on his throne.

"Proceed."

He grins at that, leaning down and taking my nipple in his mouth. I groan, and he chuckles, sliding his hand back down to the wet heat of me.

I don't think again for the rest of the night.

CHAPTER SEVEN

A^{rix}

I wake, frowning as I realize I'm hard as rock, my body wrapped around a female. I scowl. I always ensure the females I take to bed have left my chambers before I sleep.

The female in question lets out a low hum in her sleep, and I harden even further. I open my eyes, pushing aside blonde hair.

Vivian.

I'm in *her* rooms. I fell asleep with a female. This never happens.

Vivian shifts, letting out a small groan, and I run my hand over her head.

She blinks open her eyes, gazing at me blearily, as if confused that *I'm* in *her* bed.

My teeth clench.

She glances around her, as if confirming we're indeed in her room, and I narrow my own eyes.

"You're still here?" She slaps her hand over her mouth. "Sorry, I didn't mean that to sound as rude as it came out."

"Nothing dents a male's ego like being asked that very question in his own castle," I murmur, and she smirks at me.

I lean down, kissing her smirk away, and she sighs against my mouth.

"The answer is yes," I mumble, pressing kisses against her lips between each word. Then I raise myself onto my elbows, leaning over her. "I am still here because we're not done yet."

She laughs as I roll her fully onto her back. When I have her right where I want her—beneath me—I take my time, kissing my way down her smooth pale throat.

I linger over the white scar above her breast. She was almost killed during the last battle with the Dokhalls, and I tense at the memory of her, so close to death as she lay in another male's arms.

The brave female saved the life of her pregnant friend.

"Stop staring," she murmurs, and I hush her, running my tongue over her scar.

She squirms and sighs, and her needy sounds make me even harder as I take one of her nipples in my mouth. She buries her hand in my hair, holding me to her.

As if I want to be anywhere else.

Beneath Vivian's cool, calm exterior is the passion I knew was there the moment I laid eyes on her. And I'm the only one who gets to see it.

I wrestle with the possessiveness that attempts to rise at the thought, even as I'm still tonguing her nipple. I move to her other breast, playing with it until it's as hard and red as its twin.

"Beautiful," I growl. I lean up and kiss her, thrusting my tongue into her mouth. Her eyes begin to flutter shut, but she opens them at my growl. I want her to see who she is kissing. To know that while she is on this planet, no other male will make her feel this way.

I leave her mouth to retrace my steps down her neck, lingering at her breasts. I reach for one of the stockings I divested her of last night, and within moments, I have her hands tied to the wooden post above her head.

"Whoa," she says, tugging at her wrists. "What exactly do you think you're doing?"

I smile at her. "Relax, lovely. I simply don't want your hands getting in the way.

She stares at me, opening her mouth as if to protest, but her face is a picture of hopeless lust as I return my attention to her breasts, and she clamps her mouth shut.

"I thought so," I murmur.

I pinch at her nipples, enjoying the way she squirms and moans beneath me. I slip one hand down, a groan leaving my own throat at her wetness. I thrust one finger inside her, roughly pinching her nipple hard enough to make her yelp, but she clamps down around my finger, her wetness bathing my hand.

I laugh at her blush. "I wondered if you would enjoy such things, lovely."

I pinch her nipples, alternating pressure and switching between them until she's begging me.

That's more like it.

When I can wait no longer, I slide inside her, gritting my teeth as I fight not to lose control. She feels incredible around me, and I could spend all day and all night making her gasp my name.

I stroke the wonder that is the little bud between her thighs, a growl leaving my throat as she tosses her head, angling her hips for me to get deeper.

So I do.

I plunge inside her, thrusting again and again. This female steals my control, and I won't last, but I also won't fall over the edge without her.

I stroke her clit, plucking at her nipple, and then I pinch it.

"Come," I say, and she does, cursing like a dockworker as she writhes beneath me.

I choke out a laugh, but pleasure explodes up my spine as she takes me with her, and I come so hard that black dots appear in front of my eyes.

I gasp out a few curses of my own as I slump over her, careful not to crush her with my weight. When I've recovered enough to move, I untie her hands and roll, taking her with me, until she's slumped over my chest, still trembling with the aftereffects of her own pleasure.

"I find I would like one of these 'pictures' of you," I say, something close to jealousy winding its way from my stomach into my chest. "I dislike the thought of others being able to stare at your likeness whenever they please, while I will be left with nothing when you leave."

She glances up at me, her eyes wide, and I curse my mouth.

"What have you learned about the parts you need?" I ask, changing the subject.

She's still staring at me, and she clears her throat. "The problem is the control chip," she murmurs. "Alexis says we probably won't have access to all the ship's systems without it."

I nod. "You may want to ask around at the marketplace. Let it be known this is what you're looking for, and you may be surprised at who can provide it."

She studies my face for a long moment and then finally nods.

I have no doubt she will be approached. As soon as my enemies know what she is most desperate for, they are guaranteed to offer it to her. Evil people will always search for weakness, discovering what it is their target wants most and using it to purchase their loyalty.

That thought, combined with whatever possessive impulse made me admit to jealousy of those who have her "pictures," makes me gently roll her off my chest.

"I need to go," I say. "I have a meeting."

Not a lie, and my mood turns blacker at the thought. I get dressed while Vivian watches me silently, her blue-green gaze thoughtful. Her cousin has the same eyes; however, hers are often narrowed suspiciously. When the two are together, their eyes are almost identical—usually lit with mischief and crinkled with suppressed laughter.

Not for the first time, I wish my parents had given me a sibling. Someone to talk to, to strategize with. I snort at the thought. With my luck, it would likely be one more person attempting to have me killed so they could take the throne.

"I will see you later," I say, my body hardening yet again at the thought. I have never felt this level of lust for a female, and it is...disconcerting.

Vivian nods, her expression still thoughtful, and I leave, making my way toward my own rooms.

Here, I have a large meeting room, which I use for more intimate meetings with a few of my closest and most trusted advisers. Korzyn is waiting for me, and he shakes his head when he sees me. Likely, his palace spies have already reported that I slept in a female's rooms last night.

Something I have never done.

Korzyn frowns. "You took the human female to your bed."

I give him a warning look, and he narrows his eyes back at me. I sigh.

"Well, technically, I took her to *her* bed. Does this truly surprise you, Korzyn?"

His frown turns into a deep scowl. "These human females seem to be uniquely created precisely to lower the defenses of Braxian males. My sources say it has happened time and time again. Smart, fearsome warriors across Agron have fallen to their...charms."

I raise one eyebrow. "Do you have a point?"

"In the Seinex Forest close to the barbarian tribes, there is an animal called a thixis. The animal is small and unable to fight. It would be the perfect prey except for a tiny, gaseous bulb located in its throat. When it opens its mouth and blows at a predator, that predator instantly becomes as docile as a tamed karja."

I blink at him. "You are suggesting these human females are...poisoning the males here?"

"All I'm saying is it does not make any sense that these strange alien females have managed to overcome any natural Braxian resistance to outsiders."

I hear a shuffle outside the door and open it, finding Sarissa waiting. She tilts her head, and from the way she waggles her eyebrows at me, it's obvious she has heard everything he has said.

She steps inside. "I'm about to head to the marketplace," she says. "I just wanted to thank you for your help so far." She smiles sunnily at me, and I have a feeling she was in this part of the castle gathering information for her own needs.

I frown, but the female is already turning her attention

to Korzyn. She smiles, showing him her teeth, and then presses one hand to her lips before pointing it in his direction and blowing.

"What are you doing?" I ask.

"Blowing him a kiss," she murmurs. "It's something of a tradition on Earth."

Across the room, Korzyn steps back, narrowing his eyes at her. She winks at me and then struts out the door, swinging her hips as she leaves.

Korzyn raises one eyebrow at me, and I laugh.

"She is playing with you. You used to have a sense of humor."

"I can no longer afford a sense of humor if I'm going to keep you alive. Nine guards lost in one revolution, Arix. One day, you will turn a corner, and there will be no one we can trust left to protect you when someone slits your throat."

I sigh, throwing up my hands. "What would you have me do?"

"Be careful. Do not speak of anything you would not mind your enemies learning when you are close to these females. We know nothing about them."

"Fine."

We both turn at a knock on the door, and several of my advisers file in. Rachiv glances between Korzyn and me, likely noting the tension in the room, but I get straight to business as soon as everyone is seated around the large, circular table.

"Have you heard back from Rakiz about our offer?"

Tridi shakes his head. While he is not in my trusted circle, his blood relationship to me ensures his access to these meetings. Access that he always uses.

"Rakiz wants to talk in person. He says his people do not

conduct business by messenger unless there is no other choice."

"He is more than welcome to visit. We will have rooms made up for him and his mate."

"He won't leave, Your Majesty," Rachiv speaks up. "His mate is with child and close to giving birth. He made it clear he won't be leaving his tribe for some time."

I grind my teeth at that. Rakiz has something I want, and I know I have many things he would like access to on this side of the water—my marketplace in particular. Even if my offer to the human females was due to my fascination with Vivian, the fact remains that I have made the first move by giving his tribe members—temporary as they may be— access to vendors from across this galaxy.

And yet the barbaric tribe king insists I go to him?

I open my mouth to refuse, but Korzyn slides me a look, and I slam it shut, grinding my teeth. In order for our plan to work, I need access to something very particular from across the water.

"According to my spies, the human females will have the part for their thruster fixed within days," Korzyn says. "They will want to travel back to the tribe to give it to the other human females. Perhaps this would be a good opportunity to visit, while reminding the barbarian king that it is only due to your goodwill that the part is fixed."

I grind my teeth some more, but it makes sense.

"Fine. Send a messenger with our response."

CHAPTER EIGHT

V ivian

The last few days have passed in a blur of sex, sleep, and more sex. When Arix offered his terms, they sounded a lot like "be available when I need you," so I made sure to do the opposite, making him look for me all over the castle if he wanted me.

According to Sarissa, this was a good opportunity to teach him that human females aren't the type to roll over for arrogant kings.

Although, sometimes rolling over can have benefits. Especially when those benefits include coming so hard you practically forget your own name.

I blush at the thought of just how many times I "rolled over" for Arix last night.

Today, though, we're heading back to the marketplace. According to Sarissa, there's a high chance the guy who sells the part we need will be returning in the next few days.

I wince as Cauri pulls the comb through a knot in my hair, and she rolls her eyes, muttering about fragile human females.

Cauri was unimpressed when Arix left my rooms, scowling and declaring me a trollop. I pointed at the door and told her she could leave unless she was going to apologize for that remark. I may be scared of her—not that I'd ever admit such a thing to Sarissa—but that doesn't mean she gets to slut-shame me.

Cauri gaped at me, stunned, but I stared at her, waiting her out. Finally, she muttered an apology, then ordered me into the bath so she could arrange for my sheets to be changed if the king was going to be visiting them again.

I ground my teeth until I worried there would be only nubs left.

God forbid Arix roll around in the same sheets he left his spunk in.

Thankfully, he kept his word, and last night, a servant brought a tonic with my dinner. Surprisingly, Cauri nodded in approval, muttering that I may be a trollop, but at least I'm not stupid.

I let that one go.

Unfortunately, now that she knows I'm banging the king, Cauri's obsession with my appearance has reached new heights. The one good thing about the way she does my hair, however, is I no longer have flashbacks to my mother yanking on my blonde strands when I was a child. No, Cauri is worse than my mother ever was, so the dread in my stomach when I sit down at my pretty, carved vanity is entirely thanks to the maid.

It's almost ironic that Cauri's disapproving frown reminds me so much of my mother.

When I hit puberty, it quickly became evident I wasn't

going to be modeling for Chanel anytime in the future unless I had a breast reduction.

My mother bemoaned the fact I was curvier than her—eyeballing every scrap of food I put in my mouth and blaming my father's side of the family for my genes.

I actually considered it—the breast reduction. But ultimately, choosing not to go under the knife was a giant fuck-you to my mother who had been having yearly "tune-ups" since before I was born.

So I'm never going to be on the cover of *Vogue*. I have my own career, which mostly includes lingerie and swimsuit modeling. And if I occasionally wonder what it would've been like if I'd stood up to my mother and chosen my own career path...

That's no one's business but mine.

"Aren't you ready yet?"

I jolt in my seat, making Cauri curse at me. Sarissa catches my eye in the mirror, smirking, and I narrow my eyes at her.

"Almost."

"She doesn't need to look like she's going to a ball," Sarissa tells Cauri. "We're only going to the marketplace."

Cauri sniffs, sliding a jeweled pin into my hair. "Need I remind you that you are both—"

"Representing the king." Sarissa nods. "So our appearance is of utmost importance."

She says it solemnly, but her lips twitch, and Cauri frowns at her, her gaze lingering on Sarissa's hair, which is in a simple braid.

"Obviously, you haven't taken this advice seriously," she murmurs.

Sarissa nods. "I'm not the best at taking advice. Just ask my cousin. Come on, surely she's ready now?"

Cauri sighs, poking one last pin along my scalp. I grit my teeth, well aware that complaining will just make the torture last longer.

"Fine," Cauri says with a huff, and I raise my eyebrows. Sarissa has succeeded, while my complaints seem to only piss her off.

"Have you considered switching with Hesa?" I ask Cauri. "I think you'd enjoy fixing Sarissa up every day."

Sarissa smirks, and Cauri narrows her eyes at me. "Someone has to keep you in line," she says, turning to walk away. "Wear the gray shoes," she orders over her shoulder.

I linger over my shoe choices, Sarissa watching as I pick up a black pair, hesitating. Finally, I go for the gray shoes, ignoring Sarissa's snort.

"They look best with the dress."

"Uh-huh."

"I'm not afraid of her."

"Then why are you whispering?"

"In case she's still around. Duh."

The guards are waiting outside our rooms, and they murmur amongst themselves as we get into the hydro and travel down the river. The sun is still low in the sky, the air fresh, and we compete with other hydros for space as we head toward the marketplace.

"Let's see if the replacement part has arrived first, and then we can look around," Sarissa says. I nod, and we follow the path through the trees, both of us pausing as we take in the large marketplace.

Sarissa links her arm through mine. "Whatever happens, I'm glad I got to experience this stuff with you, V."

I grin at her, my eyes suddenly hot. There's no way Sarissa would be this open on Earth. An alien abduction has taught both of us that life is short.

"I'm glad too."

Sarissa smiles at me and moves toward the marketplace, but I stop her.

"Can I ask you something?"

"Of course."

"What happened when I disappeared? Did they file a missing persons report? Did they even notice?"

Sarissa's expression turns agonized, and I stare at her.

"They didn't, did they?"

"*I* did," she whispers. "I went to the police when I didn't hear from you. Your mom insisted you were probably partying overseas somewhere, and refused to get involved."

I laugh, but it comes out like a sob. "A missing daughter would be a scandal."

Sarissa sighs. "The police were looking for you, V. Your phone, wallet, and everything else were in your apartment. None of your credit cards had been used, so it was obvious you hadn't run from your life. But there was no sign of a struggle. I hired a private investigator, and I was using every contact I had to find you." Her smile is sad. "But then I woke up on that ship."

Other than our brief chat the other day when she admitted to promising the other women they'd have their revenge, Sarissa still hasn't talked about what she and the others went through on that ship.

While our group of women were only on the Dokhalls' ship for a day or so, it sounds like they were stuck in their cage for much longer. Every time I ask about her abduction, Sarissa gets a distant look in her eyes and clams up. All I know is one of the women died, and Sarissa barely held the other women together.

"Do you think you were taken because you were looking for me?"

She shrugs. "Two months after you were taken, I went to the Arcav."

My mouth drops open. "You what?"

"I'd been researching. Other women were disappearing—young, middle-class women who would be missed. But it was the same as your disappearance—no struggle, all their personal belongings at home. I approached the Arcav, and they had begun looking into it. And then I was taken."

"The Grivath knew you had alerted the Arcav. It's no coincidence that we were both taken. This is my fault. I'm sorry, Rissa."

She grabs my shoulders. "Don't be ridiculous. It's not your fault. It's the Grivath's and the Dokhalls', and we're going to make them pay."

I let out a breath I hadn't known I was holding. "Okay."

"Now let's go see a man about a spaceship."

I laugh, and we walk down the hill and into the market-place. Now that I've been here a few times, I'm not so over-whelmed by the hustle and bustle. Sarissa seems to know everyone, lifting her hand in greeting as people call her name. A blue man with thick horns calls out something in a language my translator doesn't recognize, and Sarissa responds in the same language with a laugh.

I stare at her. "Who *are* you?"

She grins but pretends to zip her lips, pointing me toward the stall we need to visit. I dodge people with fur, scales, and horns, continually shocked at how many seem to recognize my cousin.

"Ah, I wondered if you might return today," the Braxian woman says when we arrive at her kradi.

Sarissa smiles at her. "Pariv. Nice to see you. Any luck?"

Pariv nods and gestures to the kradi, where a man covered in green scales is talking to the other Braxian vendor. My heart races in anticipation as Pariv calls to him, and he turns, his yellow gaze examining us.

"This is Bacar," Pariv says before excusing herself to attend to another customer.

Bacar steps closer to us. "You are the humans looking for the part for your thruster."

"Yes," Sarissa says.

"The part from an S23 thruster, typically only flown by two races in the galaxy, the Thracias and the Dokhalls?"

Sarissa's gaze turns frosty. "Is there a problem?"

He smiles, and I tense. "No problem. Just ensuring I have the correct information."

They gaze at each other for a long moment, and his smile widens as he displays sharp, pointed teeth.

I clear my throat. "Is the part available?"

Bacar nods, never taking his eyes off Sarissa. I shiver. Something tells me that Bacar will sell us out to anyone he can at any moment.

The sooner we get off this planet, the better.

Arix's face flashes in front of my eyes, and I push it away, focusing on Bacar as he turns and strides back into the kradi. He returns a moment later with the piece we need, and Sarissa compares it to the broken piece in her hand.

Identical.

Except for the large crack in the one Sarissa is holding, of course.

"Perfect," Sarissa says. "How much do we owe you?"

They begin negotiating, and I turn as someone taps me on the shoulder.

A large man stands behind me, the sun highlighting the thick fur covering his shoulders. He reminds me of a Zinta, except his features are closer to a Braxian's.

"Can I help you?"

He nods. "Yes. And I believe I can help *you*."

Sarissa finishes up with Bacar and leans close. "What exactly do you want?"

"I have information you need. About a certain chip."

I feel Sarissa go still next to me, although her face stays blank.

"We're listening."

"Not here," the furry man says, glancing over our shoulders, where our guards are likely hanging out. "What I need to tell you must be kept secret. Those guards will ensure that anything I say reaches the commander's ears."

The man shivers. Obviously the commander has a reputation amongst the people here.

"One of us can distract the guards," Sarissa mutters, and I glance at her.

"Are you sure about this?"

"He said he has information about the chip. We have the thruster, but Alexis said we may not get out of here without the control chip, remember? At the very least, we can hear him out." She frowns at him. "But no funny business."

The man nods as if unconcerned, but his hands are trembling.

"I've got a bad feeling about this," I mumble.

"I've got this," Sarissa says. She waves her hand casually —a gesture she's used since we were kids. That gesture was always followed by something that would definitely get her put in the naughty corner. "You go listen to this guy, and I'll distract the guards."

"What? Shouldn't I distract the guards?"

She snorts. "They know you're boning the king. Your dumb blonde routine isn't going to work. They'll be too terrified of pissing off Arix."

The man's eyes widen at that, and I sigh.

"Fine."

Sarissa disappears, and I can instantly see some kind of commotion out the corner of my eye.

I turn to the furry man. "What's your name?"

He hesitates. "Varge."

Obviously that name is fake, but I shrug. "Talk."

He tilts his head, gesturing for me to follow him to the edge of the market and behind a tree. "We have access to the control chip you need."

I frown. "How? The Dokhalls took it with them."

"Not that one. The control chip is not unique to the ship and can be easily replaced. My contact has located another chip from a retired Dokhall ship on his planet. He can get it to you within days."

I narrow my eyes at him. I suddenly feel like I'm going to throw up, dread sitting like a stone in my stomach.

"In exchange for what?"

Varge grins at me. "In exchange for helping us remove the king from his throne."

CHAPTER NINE

A rix

"They took the bait," Korzyn mutters, and I ignore the way my chest tightens. I knew the human females would be approached, and I knew they would do whatever it took to get off this planet. So why is my blood heating in fury, betrayal sharp as a knife in my chest at the thought of Vivian setting me up?

I swing my sword in my hand, nodding for him to pull his own. My men have already completed their own training for the day, and I'm getting a late start.

"What happened?"

Korzyn slides his sword free. "They were approached at the marketplace, as we figured they would be. Sarissa pretended to collapse, and the guards attended her, allowing Vivian to speak to the messenger."

"Who was it?"

"Likiz, although he sometimes goes by the name Varge.

He is well known as a messenger amongst various groups. He deals in information as well."

I nod, ignoring the rage that burns through my veins. I don't know who I am angrier with—the traitors that would dare offer Vivian everything she wants in exchange for her betrayal, or Vivian herself for taking the deal.

"I'm...sorry, Arix."

I glance at Korzyn. To his credit, he looks genuinely sympathetic.

I shrug. "It was your idea to make it known exactly why the human females were here and what they needed to be able to fly their ship. We knew this would happen."

"Yes, but it is still a betrayal."

"These females are loyal to each other. Even if Vivian chose not to betray me for herself, she would still ensure that the other females could get off this planet. Do we know if they accepted?"

"The females were arguing the entire way back to their rooms, although they kept their voices low. Even if they choose not to accept now, it's only a matter of time before they agree."

Logically, I know this. If they don't agree to a deal for the chip, my enemies will likely have one of them kidnapped and held hostage to force the other to do what they want. Still, the knowledge burns.

It's ironic. The same devotion to her people and commitment to her convictions would make her an excellent queen.

Instead, she's attempting to kill a king.

I grit my teeth and nod at Korzyn, who swings at me, the power in his arm sending shock waves up my sword and into my arm as I meet his blade with my own.

I lose myself in the fight, pushing away thoughts of the female who steals my focus.

Vivian

Arix is in one hell of a mood. He's pacing my room like an angry tiger, while I stand in front of my bed, watching him.

I'm tired—both physically and emotionally—after my day at the marketplace.

I frown at Arix. "You want to talk about it?"

"No."

He can't know I was approached at the market—can he? I wouldn't put it past the commander to have put extra spies on us, but I know for sure there was no one within hearing distance when I was talking to the furry man.

Even if he knows I talked to someone, he won't know what was said.

The thought of betraying Arix makes me nauseous again. I can barely look at him as his words run through my head on a loop.

"My kingdom has its faults, and while I try to improve it every day, it will always be a work in progress. But if someone were to take it from me, I would not rest until I had taken it back. My father would expect nothing less."

The man promised that Arix wouldn't get hurt. But some things hurt worse than physical pain.

Betrayal is one of those things.

Arix's face is like stone. For whatever reason, seeing him like this makes me want to soothe him. I don't quite understand this new urge, but I shrug, swinging my legs to the side and sliding off the bed as I get to my feet.

"You know...you promised to make me scream with pleasure on a daily basis," I remind him. He whispered those words in my ear while languidly thrusting inside me just a few days ago.

He turns and tilts his head as he studies me. "You have complaints?"

He asks the question as if the idea is ludicrous, and I almost laugh. I've never been overly interested in arrogant men. I worked with some of the most attractive men on Earth when I was a model, and most of them were all ego and no real substance.

So why does *Arix's* arrogance make me wet?

"All I'm saying is you haven't fulfilled your duties today," I say. His eyes flare at the word *duties*, as I knew they would, and he prowls my way.

"I'm going to make you beg," he hisses at me, and I tense.

"Not fucking likely."

"Oh, lovely, you just ensured it."

I frown at him, but he continues advancing on me in a way that makes me feel stalked, his huge body moving like a panther.

I blink, and he's in front of me, reaching into my dress and cupping my breast. My mouth drops open, and he doesn't hesitate, taking my mouth in a deep, claiming kiss. I whimper against him, and he growls in response, running his thumb along my nipple until it's hard and aching. He touches me with ferocious urgency until I'm desperate for him.

How does he always make me feel this way? Like my skin is too tight for my body? Like I'd get on my knees for him, beg him to put his hands on me?

He gentles his lips, brushing them against mine over and over again. I reach up and bury my hand in his hair, pulling him closer, insistently. He chuckles against my mouth, turning his attention to my other nipple, and I groan as he pinches it lightly between his fingers.

His other hand is busy with the strings of my dress, and within moments, cool air hits my chest as he pushes it off my shoulders.

It falls to the floor, and I'm standing in front of him, naked.

His gaze feels like a brand as he stares at me. Then my head spins as I'm suddenly in his arms. He ignores my yelp and strides toward my bed, groaning as he lets me go, and I bounce, my boobs practically hitting me in the face. He's stripping off his clothes like they're on fire, and I push up onto my elbows so I can watch the show.

His body should be illegal. I run my eyes over his pecs and huge shoulders—not to mention the eight-pack that makes my fingers itch to touch.

"I don't get it; don't you sit around on your throne all day? How the hell do you look like that?"

He steps out of his pants, and then he's crawling up the bed until he's leaning over me. "I train with my guards every morning. It is a foolish king who relies on others to protect him."

His face hardens, and I reach up, stroking away his frown. He looks surprised for a second, and then he's leaning down, his tongue stroking against mine as I sigh against his mouth.

Within moments, he's lowering his mouth to my nipples and tonguing them, biting them, driving me crazy with *want*.

I clamp my mouth shut. *Do not beg him.*

He meets my eyes, takes my nipple into his mouth, and sucks, running his tongue against it until I want to scream.

Two can play at this game.

I moan, rubbing against him, attempting to convince him to push inside me.

He chuckles, moving away, kissing down my stomach, his hands firm and unyielding as he pushes my thighs apart. He gives me one long stroke of his tongue before plunging it inside while circling my clit with one fingertip.

Holy shit.

He brushes his finger against my wetness, moving it down, beneath my cheeks. I tense, and he moves his tongue to my clit, setting up a smooth rhythm that's guaranteed to drive me crazy. He strokes with that finger, and I open my mouth to tell him we are definitely not going anywhere near brown town, but he pokes the tip of his finger inside, his teeth scraping at my clit, and I explode from within, groaning as I twist against him, my entire body shaking.

He grins up at me as I blink at him, and then he lowers his head and begins again.

I'm incoherent within moments, too sensitive as I push him away and pull him close at the same time. He waits until I'm on the edge, and then he's moving his way up my body, positioning himself at my entrance and slowly pushing inside me.

My eyes roll back in my head, and he gives a low laugh, but it's tight, and his body is shaking as he slowly works his length into me. I raise my legs higher, spreading wide, my hands moving to his butt as I urge him on.

He doesn't hesitate, plunging into me. He hits my cervix, and I squeak. He freezes, then moves one hand down, strumming my clit as he angles his hips, thrusting again.

Oh my God.

I moan, and it seems to spur him on because he grinds against me, hitting my G-spot. There's no way I'm going to come again. Once was awesome, but twice? I highly doubt it.

"Ready to beg?"

I shake my head, but I'm already trembling around him, somehow on the edge of another orgasm. This one feels like it could be even better than the last.

He leans down, and his tongue thrusts into my mouth like he's conquering it, removing the taste of anyone who isn't him.

He slows down.

"What are you doing?"

"Beg me."

"Are you kidding?"

He winks at me. "I want to make sure you know exactly who is making you feel this way. Ask me to let you come. And make sure you say my name."

He spears into me, and I clamp down, about to teeter on the edge. I angle my hips, attempting to grind against him, and he gives me a patronizing look. He's sweating though, and it's evident he's barely holding back himself.

So why play these games?

I almost snort. Because everything between us is a game. We can't seem to help ourselves.

I won't let him win.

He smiles, as if reading my mind, and he reaches down, stroking one finger over my clit, making me gasp.

"Damn you!"

"Who is making you feel this way, lovely?"

"You are."

"Say my name."

"Arix..."

He tenses against me, growling, and then he's plunging into me, pushing me over into a climax that rips through me as I throw my head back and moan out his name.

He leans down, nips my ear, and empties himself inside me.

Arix

I'm sprawled in Vivian's bed, staring up at the ceiling. Vivian is relaxed and warm against me, slumped over my chest, her breathing even.

I have my own spies, who are currently hunting the Dokhalls as we speak. Korzyn has made it known that any Zintas found colluding with the Dokhalls will be considered enemies of my kingdom.

A small part of me wants to find the chip Vivian needs so badly just so I can destroy it in front of her.

Her betrayal hurts more than most.

She nuzzles against my chest, and I raise my hand, stroking her soft, silky hair.

"Tell me about your life," I order, still staring at the ceiling.

She shifts against me with a groan. "Sleepy."

I can't help but smile. "I want to know you."

She sighs but lifts her head, pushing her hair off her face. "There's not much to know, really. I'm not exactly close with my parents—"

"Why?" As someone who has no parents, it is difficult to understand why someone would choose not to make the most of any time they have with them.

Vivian studies my face. "You won't understand."

"Tell me anyway."

She sighs and lays her head back on my chest. "My

mother is a socialite. When I grew up, she was like one of the women in your court, I guess. Constantly at parties and dinners, all in an attempt to be seen with the right people. My father was a partner at a law firm, and he was never home. It was well known that he was constantly having affairs, and he didn't care enough to be discreet about it. This made my mom desperate for a distraction. She needed somewhere to focus her attention, and I was the convenient choice."

"Affair?"

"Sleeping with women who weren't my mother."

I frown. These human men would dishonor their mates this way?

Vivian sighs. "I was an adorable kid. At least that's what all the adults around me said. I was conventionally cute. Blonde hair, blue eyes, but most importantly, I was well-behaved. That's what they're *really* looking for in the industry when it comes to little kids. They need a fast turn-around and kids that can follow directions. So my modeling and acting career took off, and my mom became my manager. Unfortunately, I can't act my way out of a paper bag, and there's only so far looks can take you in life."

I frown. "It sounds as if your mother was living her life through you."

She nods. "As an adult, I can look back now and see what my mom was doing. When I fell in line with her plans, when I was the perfect daughter, I was rewarded with her attention. It was fleeting though. And I don't remember her ever telling me I was smart. Once, I had a nanny who told me I could go to college one day. My mother almost fired her on the spot. She said I wouldn't need college because I would be too busy traveling the world as a model. She was horrified when my breasts became too large for me to fit the sample sizes. And she's barely looked at me since the day I told her I wouldn't be getting a reduction."

I tense, sliding one hand over her breast, and she shivers. "A reduction?"

"Made smaller. They would cut here and take away some of the..." Her voice trails off as I stare at her, horrified, and she bursts out laughing.

"I think this is the most disconcerted I've ever seen you," she says.

I can barely find my words. "Your mother wanted this for you?"

She shrugs. "When I was young, it was fun, you know. As long as I was doing what I was told, my mom would be supportive, and kind...almost like a normal mom. But the moment I pushed back, she would turn on me. She could be...vicious. I know she had problems of her own—my dad was never around. But no matter how much I dieted, I was still all tits and hips. I hit rock bottom when I realized I couldn't remember the last time I'd eaten properly and I was considering going to see a surgeon. It would be one thing if it were a career I chose, or something I loved, but I was just doing it for her. And if she couldn't love me enough without the modeling, then why was I begging for scraps of her affection?"

Vivian's face is wet, and I wipe away her tears, but more quickly take their place.

"I'm sorry. Where was your father in this?"

She shrugs. "He didn't give a crap. When Mom decided she was done with me, he cut me out of his life as well. I was still modeling, but I was never going to be an editorial model, and I wasn't suitable for high fashion. I was lucky though. I had my own little niche doing commercial model-ing, and before I was abducted, I'd moved into lingerie and bikini modeling. It may not have been my passion, but I was good at it."

I don't know some of the words Vivian has spoken, but I understand a little more about her life. She was betrayed by her family and taught not to trust. She had to choose to look after herself and only herself.

Her cousin is all she has left of her family. It's not surprising that she would do anything to ensure they both return safely to their own planet.

Some of the rage that has been simmering inside of me since Korzyn told me she agreed to betray me...it is lessened. Oh, I am still angry. But I have not told Vivian I have ordered my people to search for the chip she needs. I don't want to give her false hope if it can't be found.

I scowl as thumping sounds come from the other room. Someone is banging on the door.

"Your Majesty, Your Majesty, come quick!"

Vivian's eyes widen, and she sits up, clutching her blanket to her chest. I push away the urge to order whoever has dared interrupt me to leave so I can roll her beneath me once more. Instead, I stride from the bedroom to the sitting room and throw open the door, scowling at Bevix.

His face is pale, and I open my mouth, but he's already stumbling over his words.

"It's Tridi," he says. "He's dying."

Vivian gasps behind me, and I meet her eyes. She has pulled on her dress and is leaning against the doorway.

"Stay here," I order her, and she nods as I stride from the room.

"Where is he?"

"His rooms."

I run through the halls, ignoring the gasps of the servants as they jump out of my way.

Tridi is choking on his own blood when I arrive, Korzyn attempting to stem the bleeding from his chest wound.

"He wouldn't let me call for the healers," Korzyn says. "He insisted on speaking to you first."

"Are you mad?" I turn and roar for the healers.

Bevix crouches next to me. "I've already called for them, Your Majesty. They're on the way."

I survey Tridi's chest wound as Korzyn replaces the thick cloth he's using to stem the bleeding. Tridi gasps, and I lean down.

"What happened?"

"Attack. Traitor." He coughs, and his face turns gray. "Came out of nowhere. I turned, and a knife was in my chest. The rooms were dark. I fell to the floor, and they were gone."

"You were in here?"

He nods. "Someone close. Someone with access to our rooms. Likely whoever killed your parents."

My heart sinks into my stomach, where it turns to lead. "I thought it was you," I admit. "You always looked so enraged whenever I sat on my throne."

"I know." The ghost of a smile crosses his face. "I *was* enraged. You look so much like your father. It made me sick to think he would never get to see you rule, never get to see the male you have become."

"I'm sorry."

"Don't be." He attempts a smile, but his breaths are wet. "I had a good life. Not everyone can say the same." He reaches for my hand, clutching it with surprising strength. "You need to be careful. Keep Korzyn close. Someone wants what you have, and they've killed me, they want to kill you, and they will murder anyone else who stands in their way."

"You're not dead yet." I turn, roaring again for the healers. We just need cava berries. He'll heal. He has to.

I glance back down as he squeezes my hand. He gasps, blood bubbling between his lips.

"I know a mortal wound when I see one. If I had access to a cava berry the moment I was stabbed, it might have been...different." He chokes for a moment, and I want to throw my head back and howl in frustrated fury. "I think you'll find the healers were prevented from getting here as quickly as they should have."

I glance at Bevix, and he nods.

"I'll go."

Tridi ignores that. "If the human female is the female you choose, you will need to fight to keep her safe. They will take everything you care about if you let them, Arix."

"Don't go. Please."

He smiles. "Your parents would be proud of you, boy. And I am too."

He chokes again, his body stilling, and I reach down and close his eyes.

CHAPTER TEN

V ivian

Arix is silent next to me, his eyes hard as he stares at the water as if it can solve all his problems.

Now that the part for our thruster is fixed, we're heading back to Rakiz's tribe to drop it off. Alexis and Dexar are still there while they attempt to figure out a plan to remove the threat the Dokhalls present.

Arix hasn't said much since the death of his uncle. He still comes to my rooms, but there's no more talking about our lives. Instead, he takes me again and again until I fall into an exhausted sleep. When I wake up, he is often training with his men or having meetings with his advisers.

From what Sarissa has said, not only was Arix's uncle murdered, but he and Arix were barely on speaking terms when he died. His uncle had conveniently always been around when key people were killed, and it seemed likely he was responsible for Arix's parents' deaths. But with no actual proof, Arix had chosen to allow him to stay at the castle in order to keep an eye on him. This whole time, Arix was barely tolerating him while his uncle was trying to discover the traitors himself—and ended up dead for it.

The guilt he must feel...

And the rage...

I can't do it. I can't be another person who betrays Arix. The thought makes me sick to my stomach.

Sarissa glances at me from across the boat. She's chatting to one of the guards, but I can practically read her mind. *Stay cool.*

I know it's not just about me. I know it's about the other women too. How do I sentence them to a lifetime on a planet they never wanted to land on? How do I live with myself, knowing I could have gotten that chip?

I don't. There's no way I could look the other women in the eye as we try to get off this planet. All while knowing I had the chance to get us up into space. To get revenge against the Grivath. And to get us *home.*

Maybe...maybe it's not as bad as we think. Maybe the ship doesn't actually *require* a control chip, and we can get off this planet without it.

"Are you okay?"

I blink, realizing Sarissa is now sitting in front of me. "I'm fine."

She tilts her head, but I can't bring myself to explain what I'm feeling. She *warned* me not to get attached to Arix. And now I'm considering risking all our futures just to keep his butt planted on his throne? Ridiculous.

And yet resentment sits hot and heavy in my stomach. It's easy for Sarissa. She doesn't care about anything.

I push that away. Great. A heaping spoonful of guilt has been served along with the tension and resentment. Sarissa has had an incredibly hard life. She's deeply wounded. It's not fair to blame *her* for this.

We're all silent as we get off the boat. Rakiz has arranged for some of his warriors to meet us with mishua, and from the look of the large pen they're setting up, he's obviously building some kind of stables here, which will make traveling back and forth across the water a lot easier.

Arix pulls me to him, helps me onto a mishua, and slides up behind me. I blush as Korzyn narrows his eyes at us, but he's already turning his attention to Sarissa, who is attempting to convince one of the guards to let her ride alone.

Good luck with that, cuz.

Korzyn stalks over to Sarissa and throws her over his shoulder. She curses, but he ignores her, the expression on his face making it clear she has gotten on his last nerve. He hands her to one of the guards, who lifts her onto a mishua and mounts behind her.

I almost smile as I catch Sarissa's eye. She is definitely going to make the commander pay for that little move.

She glowers at him most of the way to the camp, and it's obvious she's thinking up the best revenge. I attempt to ignore how good Arix's arm feels around my waist, but I end up slumped against his chest, falling into a light snooze.

"You were snoring," he tells me when the mishua makes a sound and I jerk awake.

"Was not," I say, feeling my cheeks heat.

He grins at me for the first time since his uncle died. I scowl, ignoring the relief that flashes through me like lightning at the sight of his smile.

"Maybe you shouldn't keep me up all night, then."

He raises one eyebrow. "Are you complaining?"

Someone makes a gagging sound, and my cousin's voice reaches my ears. "Give it a rest, you two. We're here."

Arix stares at Sarissa like she's a new, unusual species he's never seen before, and I can't help but laugh. He helps me off the mishua and strides away to speak to Rakiz, who is standing at the camp gates.

"So." Sarissa leans in close. "I've come up with a few ways to make the commander feel very, very sorry for his actions today."

She tilts her head, watching Korzyn order the guards around, and I sigh.

"Girl, you need church."

She smiles. "Wasn't there something in the Bible about doing unto others as they do to you? I liked that part."

I frown because I'm pretty sure that's not what it says, but she's already striding away, looking like she's about to start some shit.

"Viv!"

I spin, mouth dropping open. Nevada is now standing next to Rakiz, a bundle in her arms.

"Oh my God! You had the baby!"

I bounce over to her, and she laughs as I lean close.

"Vivian, meet Danica."

"Wow. She looks just like you."

Danica opens her eyes, and they're all Rakiz. "Wait. I take it back," I laugh.

Nevada pushes a blanket aside, revealing tiny, chubby baby shoulders.

"Wow." I run one hand down Danica's shoulder, gently tracing the same blue-green scales Arix and the other Braxians have, only in miniature.

My chest clenches with a longing I've never felt before.

Arix leans close, his body hard against mine as he peers down at Danica, ignoring Rakiz's obvious tension.

"You are blessed," he finally says, raising his gaze to Rakiz, who nods, satisfaction burning in his eyes as he stares at his mate and baby.

"I am," he acknowledges, meeting Nevada's gaze for a long moment. She smiles and then tilts her head, returning her attention to me.

"Now that you're back, maybe Beth will finally agree to go through with her mating ceremony. Zarix is muttering about how he's ready to tie her up and hold her down for it if he doesn't get to finally make it official soon." Nevada winks at me, and I laugh. Poor Zarix.

"Beth wants all of us there for her ceremony, and she's had a rough time. She and Alexis haven't been back to their tribe since before the last skirmish with the Dokhalls."

I smile at that, but I can't help but rub at my chest, where I now have a permanent reminder of that battle. Arix lets out a low growl next to me, his body going tense.

Rakiz steps closer. "I have had a number of kradis prepared for you," he says formally, his eyes still on Arix. "I'm looking forward to our negotiations."

Arix nods. "Thank you."

Nevada leans forward, her voice low as she murmurs to me while the Braxians discuss meeting arrangements. "You've got good timing. Alexis and Kate are planning to go see the ship tomorrow if you guys want to go with them?"

She glances behind me to where Sarissa is hanging back, stroking her hand down one of the mishua's necks. Sarissa instantly nods, and relief swims through me. If we can leave Agron without the control chip, I'll no longer be walking around feeling like I have a rock in my stomach.

"Everyone's so excited to see you guys," Nevada says, and Sarissa joins me as we follow the tribe queen into her camp.

"Zoey ordered me to make sure you guys visit her," Nevada continues. "She'll be in the healers' kradi, so let's go see her now, and then you can get some rest."

"I want to hear everything about Zoey and Tagiz," I admit, and Nevada laughs.

"Yup, the big guy didn't stand a chance against Zoey's stubbornness."

"I heard that," a voice says, and I spin, almost knocked off my feet as Zoey throws her arms around me.

"We were just coming to find you," Nevada says.

"Some of the other women are hanging out in Beth's kradi," Zoey says. "Maybe you guys can do Zarix a favor and let her know you'll be here for a couple of days. Poor guy is threatening to kidnap her if she doesn't agree to do the ceremony soon."

I burst out laughing. These Braxian males try their best to be civilized for us human women, but deep down, they'll always be barbaric warriors.

"I'll talk to her," I promise. I glance over my shoulder, and Arix nods at me as he follows Rakiz. I don't know much about their negotiations, only that Rakiz and Dexar want access to Arix's marketplace, and if I know anything about Arix, it's that he'll drive a tough bargain.

Nevada and Sarissa walk ahead, while I take my time until it's just Zoey and me.

"Do you have it?" I murmur, and Zoey nods, handing me the package I asked for.

"Be careful."

I shove the bundle deep into my pocket. "I will. Just don't tell anyone about this."

She nods again, and I smile.

"Now tell me all about how you finally got your man."

Arix

I watch the females walk away, glancing back at Rakiz to find a smile dancing around his lips as he keeps his gaze on me.

I narrow my eyes at him, and he grins. "Another Braxian falls to the charms of human females," he murmurs. Behind me, Korzyn mutters something uncomplimentary. Rakiz glances over my shoulder, his face turning hard, and I sigh.

"Korzyn is unconvinced of those charms," I murmur, and Rakiz laughs.

"As was I." He slaps me on the shoulder, and one of his warriors steps forward, directing some of my men toward their kradis.

"I've set aside some time if you would like to negotiate now? I understand if you would prefer to rest after your journey."

I almost smile at that. This tribe king believes he can taunt me into negotiating with him without a clear head. Little does he know that my father ensured I was trained for exactly this circumstance. Along with almost any circumstance imaginable.

In fact, it is to my benefit if this tribe king believes I am negotiating while tired.

"I'm willing to talk now if you are," I say, and Rakiz smiles, baring straight white teeth. I show him my own teeth, and Korzyn steps close, hand on his sword.

Rakiz glances at my commander and turns away as if unconcerned, leading us toward his tashiv. But two of the tribe king's guards fall into step between us and the king, making it clear we are not trusted at Rakiz's back.

These negotiations are already going well.

While this barbaric camp can't compare to my own kingdom, the tribe king's tashiv is large and comfortable.

A fire crackles, removing the chill from the air, and a large pile of wood is stacked neatly next to it. There are two closed doors in the tashiv, likely leading to a bathing room and a sleeping room. An older servant bustles into the room, placing a platter of food on a large table, and Rakiz gestures for me to be seated on one of the low chairs surrounding the table.

Korzyn positions himself behind me while more of Rakiz's warriors file in, joking with the tribe king and jostling as they help themselves to food before taking their own seats. I left all my advisers behind, unable to trust the people around me enough during these negotiations. Meanwhile, Rakiz is joking with one of his warriors about the male's mate, taking bets on when his babe will be born.

Is this a negotiation tactic? To make me see exactly what I'm missing in my own kingdom?

Rakiz makes one more low remark, and the other warrior throws his head back and roars with laughter. Then the tribe king focuses on me, taking his seat, his face clearing.

My mood is foul. The brotherhood here reminds me of my father's court. He hated formality, and the people he kept close were his friends.

At least most of them were.

Unbidden, I can see myself sitting next to my father, learning how to be king—and hoping I would one day be half as worthy to rule as he was. It wasn't just my father who was killed that day. My father's best friend was also found dead in another supposed accident elsewhere in the castle, as were three more of his most trusted advisers.

More of them died over the next few years, and while I built my own court, I will never be able to trust them the way Rakiz so obviously trusts his men.

The thought feels like a heavy weight on my shoulders.

Rakiz focuses on me, leaning back in his seat, and I do the same. He holds the upper hand while having these negotiations in his territory, and unless he is an idiot, he will be wondering exactly why I have not brought more of my men here.

"We want access to the marketplace," he says.

I nod. As I expected. "I want dragon scales."

Rakiz stills, and low murmurs sound from a few of his men. He glances at one of them, and the warrior nods, leaving the room.

Rakiz returns his attention to my face. "Why?"

"That is none of your concern."

I won't trust my own men with this information, let alone this tribe.

"Dragon scales are some of the most valuable goods on this planet."

"I'm aware. I am also the reason the last dragon on Agron still lives."

Rakiz nods. "We thank you for your quick action," he murmurs. "And the berries you used." From the gleam in his eye, he would also like to get his hands on some cava berries.

Perfect.

I turn my head as the door opens, and Dragix steps inside, his female by his side. Charlie, I believe her name is. She is pale, her face slightly green, and from the fierce look on Dragix's face, he is unwilling to leave her alone.

Despite the chill that comes from the wind today, the dragon is wearing nothing but a pair of pants, his gold eyes bright as they narrow on my face.

Rakiz explains what I'm looking for, and Dragix shrugs. "Are your warriors not collecting my scales as they fall?"

"I would prefer those that have not been discarded," I say. I cannot risk anything less.

Charlie narrows her eyes at me. "You want him to pluck his scales from his body and give them to you?"

I smile. "Has Vivian mentioned the many vendors who cross this galaxy to trade in my marketplace?"

Dragix glances at his female, and she frowns. They are likely having one of their silent conversations—a useful ability indeed.

"I don't want you pulling off your scales," Charlie says aloud, glowering up at the dragon.

Dragix leans forward, ignoring the many eyes on him, and his hand rises to Charlie's hair. He carefully selects one single strand and pulls it from her head, holding it up.

"Do you miss this, little two-leg?"

She shakes her head, and he smiles.

"Exactly."

Rakiz shifts, the languid movement drawing everyone's attention. "You have already given Vivian and Sarissa access to this marketplace," he reminds me.

"Yes," I say. "But they will be leaving Agron." I ignore the way my hands want to fist at my words. "I am willing to allow you to move within my territory to use this marketplace. A concession I have never made for any other Braxian tribe."

Rakiz smiles. "You must want these scales fiercely."

I smile back. "You were the one who came to *me* to provide help against the Dokhalls."

The room goes silent at the reminder. The servant squeezes between two large warriors and removes one of the trays of food, replacing it with cooked meat.

"Uh-oh," Charlie mutters. She strides to the door and opens it, and the sound of retching meets our ears. The warriors take one look at Dragix's face and don't dare jest as Charlie returns, her face gray.

Dragix pulls her into his arms, no longer amused. Time for an offer of good faith.

"I have some tea that may help your female," I murmur to Dragix.

"Standing right here," Charlie mutters, and I nod at her.

"My apologies. The tea is made from cava berries. If you sip a small cup each morning, it should help your stomach."

Charlie gives me a tiny smile. "Will it harm the baby?"

Dragix runs his hand over Charlie's flat stomach, and something like envy washes over me.

"No," I promise. "I have brought one of my healers with me. I can have her speak to your healers if you like."

Dragix nods at me, relief clear in his eyes. He turns to Rakiz.

"I give my permission for you to negotiate on my behalf," he says. Murmurs sound at this, and I barely control my expression as surprise flashes through me.

I shouldn't be surprised though. The quickest way to secure cooperation from these males is through their females.

I watch Dragix as he leads Charlie from the tashiv, my mind whirling as I adjust my strategy.

One of the other males was mentioning that his female is pregnant. Perhaps I will start there.

Rakiz is watching me intently, and I give him a bland smile.

Then I turn to the warrior at his side. "You said your female has not yet given birth?"

He tenses, his hand sliding to his sword in warning, and Korzyn growls behind me.

Rakiz glances at the warrior. "Terex," he says, and the warrior removes his hand from his sword, although it's clear he does not appreciate me speaking of his female.

I resist the urge to roll my eyes. These barbarians are exhausting to deal with.

"We have a few dried cava berries. They are not as potent as the fresh berries; however, they will last longer. I am willing to leave them with you as a show of good faith for when the time comes."

Terex turns to Rakiz. "I saw how they healed Dragix. I don't care what he wants," he says hoarsely. "Give it to him."

Rakiz sighs, sending me an unfriendly look. "You have researched our tribe well to know exactly where to strike during these negotiations."

Korzyn snorts. "It does not require research to see that your warriors are ruled by their—"

"Korzyn." I glance over my shoulder, and he clamps his mouth shut. Rakiz's smile sharpens as he studies my commander.

"Those who protest the most often fall the hardest," he says. Then he turns back to me. "You have a deal."

Vivian

"It's so nice to have you guys back for a while," Alexis says.

I smile. "It's good to be back." I glance around at the usual clearing we tend to gather in when we're all together.

Someone has thrown a few blankets on the grass, and I feel more relaxed than I have in days.

Beth bounced in place, clapping her hands, when I told her we'd be staying here for a couple of nights. Then she rushed off to find Zarix so she could let him know their mating could go ahead.

"Typical Beth." Ivy grins at me. "She doesn't care about organizing a feast or dancing; all she cares about is that we're all together."

"I know. Obviously when God was giving out sweetness, he skipped Nevada and gave it all to Beth."

Nevada grins at me as she gently sways with Danica in her arms. "That's okay. The Big Guy gave me a mean right hook."

I laugh.

I've pushed aside all thoughts of betraying Arix. Instead, I'm focusing on being in the present moment. Soon we'll go take a look at the ship, but for now, I'm going to enjoy spending time with Nevada, Ellie, Ivy, and the others. All the other women who I landed here with are going to stay on Agron. They've all found their happily ever afters.

Jealousy wraps itself around my neck and squeezes like a boa constrictor. For a second, I can't breathe, but I force myself to push it away. Each and every one of my friends fought for her happiness. And I refuse to begrudge them a single joyful moment.

None of us mention the ship that Sarissa, Alexis, Kate, Clara, and I are about to visit. Instead, we talk about inconsequential things. Danica's sleep habits. Charlie's morning sickness. Beth's mating ceremony. Zoey proudly shows off the ring Tagiz had made for her, blushing as she tells us they've decided to combine their mating ceremony with an Earth wedding for something that will be uniquely theirs. Alexis murmurs that she and Dexar are trying for a baby.

"It makes no sense in the middle of a war, but I know he'll keep us safe. Life is short, and Dexar insists he wants a bunch of kids."

I laugh at that. "And you?"

She grins. "We'll see how I deal with the first one."

I reach out and squeeze her hand. "I'm so happy for you."

"I know. Thank you."

Someone brings out a watered-down version of noptri, and anyone who's not nursing or pregnant has a few cups. Before long, the men join us, bringing more food, and the party continues as day turns into night and tribe members come and go.

It seems as if the actual negotiations have finished, and the males seem much more relaxed, most of them drinking noptri. And unlike ours, their noptri isn't watered down. Even Korzyn has a cup in his hand, and some of the tension seems to have disappeared from his face.

Sarissa stares at him like she's never seen him before, and he raises his cup as if toasting her, his gaze burning into hers as he takes a sip.

Arix is silent as he steps closer to where I'm leaning against a tree, watching as someone starts playing some music and Charlie drags her dragon onto the makeshift dance floor. She's looking much better than she was when I first arrived, the color back in her face. Dragix grins down at her, murmuring something that makes her laugh.

"This tribe is unusual," Arix says.

I glance at him, but he's staring around the clearing, his expression blank.

I shrug. "They're a family."

I follow his gaze to where Dexar and Terex are chatting to Rakiz as he holds Danica—who looks smaller than ever in his huge hands.

Nevada makes kissy sounds at her daughter and holds out her arms. He gently hands over the baby, grinning at them both.

He looks at them like they're his whole world and he'll slaughter anyone who threatens them. It's a look that's both tender and a little psychotic, and witnessing it makes my eyes sting.

Nevada pats Danica's butt and then steps closer to me.

"Here," she says, handing her to me before I can protest. "She hasn't had nearly enough time with you."

All the spit dries up in my mouth as Danica makes a tiny baby sound, kicking one of her legs beneath her blanket.

"Take her back," I hiss. "I know nothing about babies."

Nevada just laughs. "It's good practice."

"I should've known you'd be an asshole parent," I hiss. "I bet on Earth, you'd be holding up the school drop-off line while you perved on the gym teacher."

"Well, duh."

The other males go back to discussing whatever it was they were discussing, but I glance away from Danica long enough to meet midnight-blue eyes. Arix grins at me, obviously amused at my fear.

Nevada nudges me. "You look good with a baby in your arms," she teases.

"Ha ha," I mutter.

"You do," Arix says, and the amusement has left his face. We stare at each other in silence for a long moment that's broken only when Danica raises one of her tiny fists, opening her eyes and peering up at me.

"Hi," I say, and she blinks sleepily.

I sway with her, and she wraps her hand around my finger, her eyes sliding closed again. My heart melts.

Nevada grins at me. "And another one bites the dust. No one can stand strong against my daughter's charms."

I can't help but laugh, but I hold out the baby, silently pleading with her mother.

Nevada rolls her eyes but takes her from me, placing a kiss on Danica's head.

I turn to Arix, the noptri making my tongue loose. "Dance with me," I say, expecting him to refuse.

His smile is languid, and it makes my thighs clench. From the wicked look in his eyes, he knows exactly what that smile does to me.

My head spins as he takes my hand and pulls me out to the dance floor. He holds me close, swaying gently as he tucks my head beneath his chin, and I make one last desperate wish.

Please, just let it stay like this for a little longer.

CHAPTER ELEVEN

V ivian

I blink my eyes open as the kradi lightens, a low groan leaving my throat.

Too much noptri. The rest of the night after my dance with Arix is a blur, but I vaguely remember Ivy deciding the noptri would go down much easier if taken as a shot.

"Curse that flame-haired vixen and her ability to pound liquor like it's water," I mutter. From Arix's low laugh, he's feeling just fine.

I turn, attempting to keep my hungover morning breath away from his face. He ignores that, nibbling at my lips in a way that makes me wish I didn't have to get up.

"I clearly remember you challenging Ivy and Sarissa," he murmurs. "I believe you told them to 'suck your dick.'"

I groan, covering my face with the fur, and Arix laughs again, pulling it off and pressing a kiss against the tip of my nose.

He's more relaxed than I've ever seen him, his smile staying put even as I squirm away from him and reach for my clothes.

"Where are you going?" he asks.

I sigh at the grass stains all over my dress. Cauri is going to kill me.

I glance up at him. "I haven't had a good look at the ship yet. Alexis wants to take the thruster part to the ship and make sure it fits. Dexar has agreed, and he's coming with us, along with half his army." I roll my eyes, and Arix's smile drops from his face.

"Be careful."

I ignore the warmth that blooms in my chest at his warning. "What will you do today?"

"We'll solidify the terms of my agreement with Rakiz's and Dexar's tribes." I suppress the urge to ask him exactly what those terms are. If he wanted me to know, he would've told me.

Fling, V. He doesn't need to tell you shit.

I glance back down at the dress and shrug. I'll change later before Beth's mating ceremony. Arix watches me through dark eyes as I pull it on, and I run a comb through my hair. My hands still as I realize how much I've cut down my morning routine.

Usually, I'd feel the need to darken my lashes, contour my cheekbones, and stain my lips. But for some reason...the thought hadn't occurred to me this morning.

My head spins as I get to my feet, and I gulp down some water, hoping it'll take care of the headache that's currently pounding behind my right eye. I groan again as I open the kradi flap and the sun hits my face.

Arix's chuckle reaches me, and I scowl over my shoulder at him.

"You could have some sympathy, you know."

"I told you to slow down. You called me a 'pussy.'"

I groan again and step out of the kradi, finding Alexis, Kate, Sarissa, and Clara waiting for me.

Alexis is the only one who looks fresh-faced, while Kate and Sarissa are both squinting into the sun as if it has personally offended them. Clara's face is so pale that her freckles are stark against her skin.

At least I'm not the only one who's hungover like a dog.

Alexis smirks at me, running her eyes over the other two women. She opens her mouth, and I glower at her.

"Don't even start."

Her smirk turns into a grin, but she gestures at the guards who'll be traveling with us, her face turning serious. Dexar is waiting with them, and from the look on his face, he's not exactly excited about taking us with him.

His eyes scan the guards, who all straighten under his attention. Finally, he murmurs something to them, and Korzyn steps up next to us.

"What are you doing here?" Sarissa mutters, holding up her hand in a bid to protect her eyes from the sun.

"Arix ordered me to go with you."

From the scowl on his face, he's feeling just as terrible as we are, and Sarissa gives me a satisfied grin as we head toward the mishua.

We're mostly silent as we travel toward the ship, passing the time with our own thoughts. Kate's face is grim, and I know she's worried about being responsible for so many lives.

Finally, the huge ship comes into view, and we all take a moment to stare at it silently.

It's a shock to the system, seeing the futuristic silver spaceship in front of us. It's designed in a *V* shape, with the bridge and main hull in the point of the *V* and what Alexis says are hangars at the two ends of it.

I stare at the rows of windows, imagining myself standing on the ship, looking out at the deep blackness of space.

Butterflies are wild in my stomach as we leave the men to guard the outside of the ship and walk up the steps. Are we seriously going to be able to fly this thing into space? Where one mistake can cost us our lives?

Thankfully, I won't be responsible for keeping everyone else alive. Alexis and Kate are already having an intense conversation about the ship as Clara, Sarissa, and I follow them into the area Alexis referred to as the "bridge."

They get to work, pressing a few buttons, murmuring amongst themselves, while I wander the bridge, keeping my hands firmly behind my back as I examine the multitude of bright lights and weird-shaped buttons.

Sarissa leans against a wall and watches them work with keen eyes. She'll likely ask to be taught everything Kate knows, just in case Kate is ever out of action.

Kate flicks a switch, and I gasp as a hologram appears in the flight deck, highlighting various charts, graphs, and numbers. Kate and Alexis mutter some more, still pressing buttons in an order that makes sense only to them.

Clara moves closer to me and Sarissa. "I wanted to thank you both for what you're doing."

I raise an eyebrow, and she tilts her head, lowering her voice even further. "Sarissa told me you've made a deal to help us get a control chip."

Fury burns through me, and I can't even look at my cousin. I can feel her eyes on me, but I refuse to meet her gaze.

"Please," I say. "Don't mention it."

Clara's brow creases in confusion. "I know it must be difficult over there, so far from your friends, but I wanted to let you know how much I and the other women appreciate it." Her eyes turn sad. "I was supposed to graduate college the day after I was taken."

My mouth tastes like ash. "What were you studying?"

"Political science. I was the first in my family to go to college. My parents were so proud. Now they probably think I'm dead."

"I'm so sorry."

Clara shrugs. "We all have our stories. None of them are good. That's why I'm looking forward to getting off this planet. Maybe we'll be able to find a way to contact Earth. At the very least, we might be able to give our families some hope."

My stomach swims, and I take a deep breath as I finally meet Sarissa's knowing gaze. This is what we're fighting for. These women who've had everything taken from them.

Kate lets out a triumphant sound and hits a blue button, and we all jump as a smooth female voice sounds, speaking a strange language.

"My translator isn't picking that up," Alexis frowns. "Is anyone else's?"

I open my mouth, but the voice cuts me off.

"Language detected. Human. English. Please insert control chip for full access to flight capabilities."

Kate frowns, and Sarissa snorts. "You mean the control chip we don't have?"

"Please repeat your question."

We all freeze, and Alexis clears her throat.

"Computer, access last known flight path."

"Access denied. You may not access any functions in that category. Please insert control chip."

I can practically hear Alexis grinding her teeth. Kate grins at her.

"Access weapons systems," Kate says.

"Access denied. You may not access any functions in that category. Please insert control chip."

"Access flight systems," Alexis tries.

"Access denied. You may not access any functions in that category. Please insert control chip."

"Access startup systems," Kate mutters.

"Accessing...please hold...systems accessed."

My heart flutters in my chest.

"Access primary controls," Alexis says.

"Access denied. You may not access any functions in that category. Please insert control chip."

"For fuck's sake," Sarissa murmurs. "What *can* we do?"

"You may access environmental systems."

Alexis lets out a long-suffering sigh. "Display environmental systems."

"Environmental systems displayed. Please select your preferred temperature."

Is it just me, or does the computer sound...smug?

"Great. We can change the fucking temperature," Kate mutters, and Alexis laughs.

Alexis and Kate study the holo-screens in front of them, and I sidle close enough to examine them. They're now in English, yet I still have no idea what they actually mean.

Alexis frowns. "Computer, please list current accessible functions."

"Functions not available. Please state your desired action."

"Access fuel systems."

"Fuel systems displayed."

"Well, we can also see how much fuel we have. That's something," Alexis mutters.

"Explain this to us like you're explaining it to a six-year-old," Sarissa orders.

Kate glances over her shoulder.

"It's not great," she says. "We may be able to get off the ground with the secondary systems, but we can't use any of the ship's weapons, which would make us sitting ducks in space. I'll need to spend at least a few hours in here to understand exactly what we can use, but..."

"We'd be taking a massive risk."

Alexis snorts. "Getting on this ship *with* the control chip is a massive risk. You have no idea what you're going to find out there. Using it without full access to the systems? It's suicide."

I swallow. "Well, that's depressing."

Alexis shrugs. "You know what else is depressing? Getting off Agron only to end up being blown to pieces or lost in space."

"She has a point," Sarissa mutters, and I sigh.

We're even quieter on the way back, all of us deep in thought. The guards are tense, and Korzyn insists on going ahead a few times so he can check for any potential ambushes.

The fresh air seems to help clear my head, and I feel slightly more alert when we get back to camp, although I'd give almost anything for a nonfat vanilla latte. We head straight to Nevada's tashiv, where the guys have been kicked out and most of the women are congregating.

Beth smiles as we walk in. "Viv, I have a favor to ask. Will you—"

"Help you get ready?" I finish with a grin. "Of course."

Sarissa frowns slightly at that, and I realize she hasn't

been here for any of the other mating ceremonies. Ivy grins from where she's sitting in one of the low chairs near the fire, a cup of noptri in her hand.

"Hair of the dog," she says at my raised eyebrow, and I laugh. She turns to Sarissa. "Vivian is our unofficial makeup artist and hair stylist. She works miracles."

Sarissa nods, a weird look crossing her face, and I slump into one of the empty chairs by the fire, opening my mouth to ask her what's up. Nevada takes the opportunity to hand Danica to me, laughing as I freeze in place.

"You're looking at a baby, not a firing squad. Relax."

I glower at her, but I lean back in the chair, sniffing at Danica's head.

Ivy leans closer, and we both inhale. "That new baby smell is addictive. Better make sure you're being careful with that hot king."

I groan as the other women crack up. The door opens, and Ellie waddles in, a deep scowl on her face.

"What's wrong?" I ask, and she gives me a half hug in greeting, wrapping her arm around my shoulder as she coos at Danica.

"I'm still pregnant! That's what's wrong!" she wails, and Nevada laughs.

"It'll happen."

"It feels like I'm going to be this big forever!"

"How many women do you know who've just stayed pregnant for the rest of their lives?"

Ellie scowls. "I don't need your logic, Miss *I Have a Cute Little Bowling-Ball Belly, and I'm Going to Have My Baby Early So She Doesn't Ruin My Vagina!*"

Nevada simply grins, raising her eyebrow. "That name has a certain ring to it. You know I didn't exactly plan any of that, right?"

"I'm the size of a house!"

I kiss the top of Danica's tiny head, hiding my smile. Ellie is short, and right now, she's all belly.

"I'd be pissed too," I say. "You got pregnant before Nevada. Trust her to beat you to the push."

Nevada smirks at me. "I can't help biology." She turns to Ellie. "Maybe you need to relax. You know, light some candles, hang out in your kradi...bow chicka wow wow."

Ellie stares at her. "Yeah. Because I feel so sexy right now."

We crack up as Charlie walks in. She obviously overheard Ellie, because she's also grinning. "Are you seriously telling me Terex wouldn't jump you if you raised an eyebrow his way? He looks at you the way I used to look at candy."

Ellie blushes at that. "It's hard to feel sexy when you're so large you could have your own zip code."

"Well there are no zip codes on Agron," Nevada says. "And Terex has made it clear he can't get enough of you. Sex can bring on labor—everyone knows that. Have a few orgasms, eat some spicy food, and the baby will be here before you know it."

Ellie sits down, looking a little more relaxed. "I'm sorry, you guys. I know I'm being ridiculous."

Nevada snorts. "Don't let Zoey hear you say that."

"Too late," a voice says, and I glance over my shoulder as Zoey walks in.

"You know, that's becoming a habit," I murmur.

I glance at Ellie, and she blushes again.

"A few weeks ago, I had a meltdown. There were rumors going around that human women weren't large enough to birth Braxian babies. I was convinced I was going to die. Don't worry," she says at the look on my face. "I feel much better now."

I scowl. "And who exactly started these rumors?"

Because I'll make them pay.

Nevada grins at me, leaning over to check on her daughter as she gurgles. "I like where your mind's at, but Zoey already gave them a verbal beatdown."

I glance at Zoey, who turns an even darker shade of red. "Seriously?"

Ellie's lips twitch. "Yup. I heard it was something to see. And hear. She alluded to the fact she's in charge of poisons, so people shouldn't piss her off. Apparently, it was glorious."

Zoey smiles as we all stare at her. "Oh, it was."

"Wow, I've missed a lot." My heart pangs.

But I wouldn't take my time with Arix back for anything.

"Right." I turn to Beth. "Let's get you ready so you can blow your man's mind."

Arix

Vivian looks like a queen.

I know I should be looking at Beth, the female who is currently walking toward her mate, her joy almost blinding. Zarix stares at her as if it takes all his willpower to not stride across the large clearing and pull her into his arms.

But my gaze is continually drawn to the female next to me, her hair falling below her shoulders in soft waves. She has done something to darken her eyes, and they practically glow as she swipes away a tear, laughing as Zarix forces his hands behind his back in an obvious effort to prevent himself from dragging his mate to him.

Beth's smile widens, and she steps onto tiptoe, pressing a

kiss to Zarix's chin. Vivian sighs, and I force my attention away from her, glancing around the large clearing instead.

Beth isn't a member of this tribe, but she and Zarix are obviously well liked. Not only have tribe members traveled from Dexar's tribe to be here, but most of this tribe are squeezed shoulder to shoulder in what previously seemed like a huge space.

Dexar grins at the couple, his gaze lifting to where his own mate stands close by. She winks at him, and that grin widens, filled with promise.

The fire burns behind them, and within moments, Dexar has thrown Beth over the fire and into her mate's arms.

What would it be like to have a female of my own? I reach for Vivian's hand before I can stop myself, and she glances at me, her eyes widening slightly in surprise before she smiles at me and returns her attention to the mating ceremony.

I have long known that I must eventually take a mate. But unlike my parents with their love match, I have no desire to risk losing a true mate to the traitors that are aiming for my throne. My mate would be targeted by those who would never want to risk another heir in line for the throne, and any match must be with a female who will be willing to take that risk and be rewarded accordingly.

Likely one of the sycophants in my court who will be happy to sit on the throne, even if it means it's the last thing they do.

I have no illusions about my ability to protect a female. My parents thought they were well protected, and my father trusted his guards to keep my mother and me safe.

Vivian squeezes my hand, and I glance at her. She's

frowning slightly, and I realize I've tightened my hand on hers.

I raise it, pressing my lips to her wrist in apology.

Javir, the boy the couple treat as a son, stands next to Zarix, his shoulders straight. He hands two gold bands to Zarix, who takes them, his words loud and clear as he keeps his gaze on Beth's face.

"My brave female. I have made these bands to represent our bond. Strong, true, and never to be broken. Will you accept them?"

"I will."

Beth repeats the words, and I raise my eyebrows as she ties her own bands onto Zarix's wrists.

Zarix doesn't hesitate. Within moments, Beth is in his arms, his mouth on hers.

The rest of the night passes in a blur of food, music, and noptri. Vivian is quiet, something obviously on her mind, but I don't ask what she is thinking.

I'm not sure I want to know.

***

Vivian

I wake to warm hands on my body, and I stretch languidly, a sound almost like a purr leaving my throat.

My eyes open and meet dark, fathomless blue. My breath catches in my throat, and I raise my hands, burying them in Arix's dark hair.

Beautiful man.

He smiles down at me, but the smile is sad. For whatever reason, it hurts something in my chest to see sadness on his face, and I grin up at him mischievously.

"Well, Your Majesty, you have me right where you want me. Now what are you going to do with me?"

His grin is a dark promise, and I shiver.

Deft fingers begin undoing the dress I fell asleep in, and I sigh as one of his hands moves down to my breast, playing with my nipple until it's hard and aching.

I let out a strangled moan, and he pushes the furs away, his eyes burning as he helps me out of my dress. When my chest is bared for him, he lowers his mouth, closing it over my nipple, lightly running his teeth over it until I'm squirming against him.

He laughs and moves to my other breast, sucking at my nipple until it's throbbing and I'm pleading with him between breathless gasps.

I hold his head against me, and he growls as I pull at his hair. His mouth is hot as he kisses his way up my neck until it finally slants over mine, his lips demanding, his need clear.

I open my mouth, moaning at the taste of him. This man, who was always supposed to be a casual fling, tastes like sin and hope.

He reaches down and pushes my legs apart impatiently, and I run my hands over his bare chest, enjoying the way he tenses against me. My fingers dance over the bumps and ridges of his abdomen, his muscles flexing as I move my hand lower.

He catches my wrist with a laugh. "I don't think so."

His mouth moves lower again, and my thighs clench as his tongue is suddenly probing me, licking, sucking, and tormenting me.

This man enjoys making me go out of my mind with lust, and a strangled sob leaves my throat as one hand moves beneath my butt, lifting me so he can bury his tongue even deeper. He moves up, flicking at my clit, and his finger joins the party, thrusting into me as he nibbles at my clit.

I dissolve around him, my hands scrambling across his shoulders, nails digging into his skin. His low growl tells me he enjoys that, and I arch with desperate need as he finally moves between my legs, his mouth covering mine.

I moan against his lips as he thrusts into me, my nails raking down his back. He moves deeper, angling my hips until he hits that spot that drives me wild.

I clench around him. "Faster."

His grin is wicked as he slows down instead, grinding against my clit with every thrust. He pulls back until he almost leaves me completely but then slams into me, making me shudder in bliss.

My eyes drift closed, and I force them open, finding his gaze on my face.

"Again," I order him, and he smiles, but I can see from the tension on his face that he's barely holding on to his control.

"You're not in charge here, lovely."

I scowl, but he does something with his hips that makes me gasp and clench around him. That makes him growl, so I do it again, and again.

He moves then. Long, deep strokes that drive me insane while he gazes down at me, his eyes shuttered.

Even now, we can't be honest with each other, and I slam my own eyes closed.

He nuzzles my ear, and I moan as his new position ensures his pubic bone is hitting my clit with each thrust.

"Open your eyes," he murmurs, and I do, finding his blazing with male challenge. I lift my hips, wrapping my legs around his waist, and his jaw tightens.

He strums his fingers over my clit, and I cry out as I'm suddenly engulfed in overwhelming pleasure.

He murmurs something I can't hear, burying his face against my neck as he shudders against me.

I raise my hands to his head, clutching tight. Since his uncle's death, Arix has left immediately each time we slept together, and I half expect him to get up and find his pants. But instead, he rolls onto his back, dragging me with him.

"Alexis managed to connect the fixed part of the thruster to the thruster itself, and it's now in working order," I murmur. "I know I've said it before, but thank you."

He shrugs, but I mentally curse myself for bringing up the subject as his body tenses against mine, his brow lowering. I slide one hand along his chest, scratching my fingernails across his nipple.

"Wicked female."

I laugh at that, and some of the strain leaves his face.

"So what do you think of Rakiz's tribe?" I ask lightly.

He's quiet for a long moment, his hand stroking my hair. "I've...enjoyed my time here. The relationship he has with his warriors reminds me of the way my father interacted with his guards and advisers when he was still alive." His voice doesn't change, but his eyes are dark when he speaks of his dad.

"You seem to be close to your warriors."

He shakes his head. "There can be no true relationship without trust," he murmurs. "My parents' murders taught me that. They were kind, fair rulers who trusted those around them. And that trust killed them. Rakiz should be careful that the same doesn't happen to him."

I can't imagine anyone betraying Rakiz. But as Alexis found out when one of Dexar's guards handed her over to his enemy, no king is exempt from betrayal.

"You said your mom loved her gardens. What did your father love?"

He smiles. "My mother. He doted on her every whim. Rumors were constantly flying about how he would do anything for his queen. It was seen as a weakness, but he didn't care." His smile disappears. "He should have."

"It sounds like they were happy."

He nods. "Watching my father love my mother was illuminating. He was devoted to her. Some say that devotion made him shortsighted. He wasn't as careful as he should've been when it came to his guards."

My mouth goes dry. "You were supposed to be there that night."

"Yes. It was my inability to stay where I was told that saved my life. And cost my parents theirs."

I frown. "You were just a kid. You couldn't have saved them."

"There are secret passages throughout my castle. Most of them had been forgotten, many of them blocked off, as they were too dangerous. But I loved to explore in my free time. If I'd been in the royal quarters, I could have saved my parents."

My heart aches for the little boy who was supposed to be murdered with his parents that night. "You might have died with them."

"Or they might have lived." He shrugs. "There's no way to know now."

I open my mouth, frowning as Arix shrugs again, the picture of indifference.

But I see beyond that indifference now. And he's a man who's swamped in pain.

I lift myself onto one elbow and stare at him.

I can't believe I thought Arix had no feelings. He's

bursting with feelings. Just because he hides them behind a charming grin and a lewd mouth doesn't mean they don't exist. And he's been missing his parents every day since they were taken from him.

"What is it?" he asks, running his hand over my back.

"Nothing." I lower my lips to his, hoping his taste will replace the ashy taste of betrayal that has filled my mouth. "Nothing at all."

CHAPTER TWELVE

V ivian

I study the vendors disinterestedly, ignoring the way my stomach rumbles at the smell of the roasted nuts I love.

We're back at the marketplace after traveling from Rakiz's camp yesterday. Truthfully, between the happiness radiating from all my friends and the weight of the hope in the other women's eyes, it was almost a relief to leave.

Now, though, the castle is full of Braxians from a tribe bordering Arix's territory. He obviously needs to keep them on his side, because he's been spending hours negotiating with them.

"What exactly are we looking for?" Sarissa asks.

"I'll know it when I see it."

I don't want to admit to Sarissa exactly what I'm doing. Because it'll be an admission that I care more for Arix than I should.

She shrugs. "Varge said he'll meet us in the same place he spoke to you last time."

I grind my teeth but nod. That's the reason we're truly here. To collaborate against the man who shares my bed each night.

For whatever reason, our guards are no longer sticking as close as they used to, giving us more freedom. Freedom that Sarissa is taking full advantage of. In fact, we have our own little side project that may help lessen the sting when Arix is ousted from his throne.

A project that may help him get that throne back.

Yeah, because he's really going to forgive you and listen to what you have to say. And he's definitely going to trust any other information you give him after you've stabbed him in the back.

"Are you okay?" Sarissa asks, and I shrug.

"Fine."

She raises her eyebrow but chooses not to say anything, and we walk through the marketplace in silence. It's no longer an interesting, almost magical place for me. Instead, it represents betrayal.

Bright colors catch my eye, and I can't help but stop in my tracks. A woman with green skin slams into me and hisses something my translator doesn't catch, her elbow hitting me in the ribs as she strides past me. I ignore her, staring at the paintings.

"Wow," I murmur, and Sarissa silently follows me as I walk closer to the vendor's kradi.

The colors aren't as bright or as vivid as those I've seen on Earth. They're more...muted, but no less beautiful. In fact, the sheer skill it must require to paint these without access to the types of paints and brushes we have...

"Incredible."

The paintings depict scenes from across Agron. In one of them, an old man with horns sits on a porch in a forest, looking content, if a little lonely. In another, a dragon flies above the Colossal Water at sunset, his reflection shimmering below.

"That's Dragix," I murmur, and Sarissa nods.

"Look at that one." She points, and my heart flips. Arix is wearing a midnight crown as he lounges on his throne. He's looking down at someone, his brow creased slightly in thought, one corner of his mouth curled up and his long fingers wrapped around a jeweled cup.

My heart stutters. I *need* that painting.

I tune out everything and everyone around me, turning to the vendor, who has been watching me closely. He's scaled, the red-and-pink colors blurring together in a way that makes me dizzy, his eyes a bright gold.

"Are you the painter?"

He shakes his head. "My brother."

"Will you give me his information?"

He shrugs but finally rattles off the details. I glance at Sarissa, who sighs but pulls out one of her pieces of paper and writes down the guy's name and address.

The vendor tilts his head. "He will be here tomorrow if you would like to meet him."

I definitely would. For now, I point to the painting of Arix. I don't care how, but I'm taking that thing with me when I leave.

"How much?"

He names a price that makes Sarissa choke, and I narrow my eyes at him.

"How much if we weren't human?"

He smiles, displaying crooked yellow teeth. "Your race has nothing to do with the price."

I scowl. "What is it, then?"

"The look on your face when you gaze at our king."

I blush, and Sarissa tuts, a smirk playing around her mouth. "Someone's dick-struck," she mutters, and I wish the ground would open up and swallow me.

I stare at the vendor, who sighs.

"Since you obviously plan to give my brother more work, I'll take ten credits."

"Seven."

"Nine, and I'll have it delivered to the castle."

I raise my eyebrows at that, and he laughs. "Everyone knows of the strange females staying as the king's guests."

I sigh but dig into my pocket and hand them over. Arix insisted we never leave without a pocketful of credits, so technically, he's the one buying this painting for me. Since he's the reason I feel the need to buy it in the first place, it seems fitting.

I'm in a better mood as we walk away. Sarissa wisely chooses not to mention the fact my "fling" is veering into dangerous territory.

Next, I'll probably be cutting off a lock of Arix's hair to take with me when I get on that ship.

Actually, that's a great idea.

No, no, no. This was always meant to be temporary. I was supposed to have some fun and get him out of my system. I need to get a handle on whatever obsession I seem to have with the man.

I hesitate, about to whirl around and stalk back to the vendor to tell him I don't want the painting after all.

Sarissa nudges me, murmuring under her breath. "There he is."

Shit.

I walk toward Varge as if I'm walking toward the gallows. Apparently, Sarissa has already arranged for our guards to be distracted for the next few moments. She now has enough contacts in this kingdom to run all kinds of plans. It's a little scary, to be honest.

"Greetings," Varge says. He runs a hand over his furry head and nods at Sarissa as she steps closer.

"There will be a ball in six nights," he says, getting straight down to business. "Nobles from many tribes across this part of Agron will be attending with petitions for the king. All you have to do is ensure he is in a particular place at a particular time."

Sarissa narrows her eyes at him. "How exactly will this work? You promised the king won't get hurt."

He nods quickly. "My contact is planning to overthrow the king with evidence of his ineffectual rule. He will convince the council he should rule in Arix's place."

It takes everything in me not to punch Varge in the face.

"We want the chip first," Sarissa says, and he laughs.

"If you have the chip, what will compel you to hold up your part of the deal?"

"If we hold up our part of the deal, what will compel you to give us the chip?"

Stalemate.

Varge sighs and turns to Sarissa. "We will meet you at the dock on the night of the ball and will give you the chip." He nods at me. "You will help us overthrow the king and will then be free to go."

I glance at Sarissa, who frowns.

"We'll think about it and let you know."

Varge scowls at that, his huge, furry eyebrows drawing together like two giant caterpillars. "We don't have much time."

"We'll get a message to you. Who should we use at the castle?"

I hold my breath, wondering if Varge will actually tell us. He hesitates and then finally shrugs.

"Give it to your maid," he tells Sarissa, and I stiffen. Arix is surrounded by traitors.

"Done." Sarissa nods as if completely unconcerned, and Varge turns and walks away.

"Are you going to be able to do this?" Sarissa asks me.

"Do you want my honest answer?"

"Of course."

"I think this is all a mistake."

Sarissa's silence almost makes my ears bleed.

"Okay," she finally says. "How do *you* suggest we tell everyone we can't actually get off this planet because you lost your lady balls?"

I inhale so sharply I almost choke.

"Oh, of course it's so easy for you," I snap. "You don't give a shit about anything or anyone!"

She stares at me, hurt, and then fury flashes in her eyes. "You really think that?"

I throw up my hands. "Arix has been good to us. Better than good. He didn't have to let us stay with him. We have our thruster fixed because of him."

She rolls her eyes. "Get a grip, V. He didn't do that out of the goodness of his heart. He did it because he wanted to fuck you. How are you not used to that by now?"

I flinch. "Regardless of *why* he did it, he doesn't deserve to lose his throne."

"And we didn't deserve to lose our home! Do you honestly still think life is *fair*? Life sucks, Vivian! You can have your moral dilemma all you want, but it's not going to change the fact we have thirty women depending on us to get that fucking ship in the air."

I open my mouth, but she holds up her hand, her eyes burning.

"Those women had lives and families and homes that were ripped away from them. You may be getting starry-eyed over that man, but you know deep down he's not going to lose any sleep when you leave. He'll move straight on to the next woman, and the next after that. He's broken, V."

That's it. The gloves are off. "You want to point fingers at Arix?" I laugh coldly. "You're willing to betray *anyone* to get what you want. You're broken too!"

She nods, her lips bloodless. "I am. But I don't pretend to be anything I'm not. You made a choice. So either honor that choice or don't, but don't stand there and judge me for doing whatever it takes to make things right for those women. And don't you dare pretend you didn't know exactly what you were signing up for when we agreed to this deal."

"He's a good ruler, Sarissa. He does good things here. You don't care that he'll lose his throne and this place might end up in a civil war?"

"I was a good person too, once. Those women who had their lives taken from them are good people. Being a good person means nothing in this universe. If you can't play your part in this, let me know, and I'll do it myself. But don't fool yourself into thinking your hands won't be just as dirty as mine."

We stare at each other in silence, and I blink back tears.

When we were kids, we saw each other intermittently. Our moms were constantly fighting, and it could be years before they made up from their last fight and had a big dramatic reunion scene. Then we'd be sleeping over at each other's houses every weekend for months, until the next fight occurred.

We swore that would never happen to us. But I don't know if I can ever recover from this.

Because as tempting as it is to blame my cousin for this, it's not her fault. All she's doing is holding up a mirror. I want Arix to love me. I want him to keep his throne. But I also want revenge. And I want the other women to get off this planet and live the lives *they* want to live. I want everything, but I don't want the consequences that come along with any of the choices I have to make.

It's easier to blame Sarissa when she's the only one strong enough to make the hard choices and deal with those consequences.

The way she's been doing all her life.

She tilts her head as if reading my mind, and then she turns and stalks away.

CHAPTER THIRTEEN

Vivian

I'm in a terrible mood when I arrive back in my rooms, finding Arix lounging on my bed.

"Don't you have things to do?"

"I do." His grin makes it clear that I'm one of the things he has to do.

I slump down beside him, my head hitting the soft blankets with a thump. He leans over me and gently rubs his lips against mine.

"I know what happened at the market today."

I break out in a cold sweat. "I can explain."

He grins. "Explain how you bought a painting of me? You don't need a painting, lovely. You have the real thing."

My heart almost breaks at his words, and my face must fall, because he frowns. "What's wrong?" He takes my hands, and his frown deepens. "You're cold as ice."

I force out a laugh, ignoring the question. "I couldn't help myself. The painting captured you perfectly. You looked like you were contemplating doing something you knew was wicked but you'd definitely enjoy the process."

He smiles and leans closer, murmuring into my ear, "If I remember correctly, the last time I allowed someone to draw me was the day I met you."

I shiver, and my eyes widen as he moves away. I wish I could paint so I could capture the way he looks right now.

His eyes are as dark and mysterious as midnight. But the warmth in my chest when he looks at me is as bright as dawn and just as hopeful.

Sorrow makes my hands shake, and his eyes narrow on me.

"I know what will make you feel better."

I glance at his lips, my nipples hardening. He laughs.

"Not that, my wicked female. Come with me."

He gets to his feet, and I frown, following him out of the room, down the hall, and out a back entrance of the castle. Guards trail at a distance, but he waves away any advisers that approach, leaving Rachiv staring after us.

"What's this?" I ask.

"This is where I come to relax."

I watch as he picks up a crossbow, loading it with an arrow and handing it to me.

He gestures at the target in the distance. "It will make you feel better. I promise."

I shrug and aim, the arrow hitting the target with a *thack*.

Arix stares at me, more surprise than I've ever seen on his face.

"My guards mentioned you won a game at the marketplace, but this..." He turns and walks closer to the target, which must be twenty feet away. He studies it and then walks back to me, pointing at the next target, which is further away.

I hit it and load another arrow before hitting it again. The movement becomes repetitive as Arix guides me to the next target, and the next.

A crowd gathers, but I tune them out, fury and frustration warring within me.

I can't do this anymore.

The thought slams into me like an asteroid. I can't look at this man, can't kiss him while knowing I'm going to betray him.

There's an animal in Australia called a quokka. When threatened by a predator, it'll relax its pouch muscles, allowing its baby to fall out. The baby will lie on the ground, hissing and drawing the predator's attention so the mother can escape.

Most people would agree that's cold. But what if the sacrifice of those babies means the survival of the species as a whole?

Arix somehow snuck beneath all my defenses. But how do I give up the futures of the women who are so desperate to get home?

Strong hands take the crossbow from me, and I blink, realizing my face is wet. Arix's eyes are dark, his face hard as he waves his hand, and the people gathered around us begin to thin out.

"It's not as bad as you think it is," he says, and I choke out a laugh.

He wipes my tears, and I open my mouth, ready to tell him everything.

"Your Majesty."

We both turn at Bevix's voice. Arix's expression goes cold at the interruption, and Bevix bows his head.

"It's Korzyn. He was attacked."

Arix

Korzyn is unconscious but alive. He's deathly pale, but he has traces of blue around his mouth. My knees go weak as I slump into the chair next to his bed.

"He was carrying cava berries," I murmur, and the healer nods.

I resist the urge to slide my hand into my own pocket, where a few of the dried berries are hidden. Korzyn's planning and paranoia have saved his life.

"The berries began the healing process, giving us enough time to get to him. Once again, we were detained," the healer says, and I tear my gaze from Korzyn, meeting her eyes.

She nods at whatever she sees on my face. "The main door leading to the healers' quarters was barred. Sevis—one of the younger healers—managed to climb out a window, reaching your commander just in time, while the rest of us were forced to wait for some of your guards to break down the door."

She shivers and glances at the wreckage of the door.

"You did well," I manage to get out, my hands fisting. Sevis will be rewarded for her quick thinking.

The traitors are getting desperate. My spies are up against their spies, and they know for sure that Korzyn would never betray me.

My mind flashes back to the moment I first sat on my father's throne. I felt overwhelmed, horror and anguish warring within me, while I fought to keep my face blank.

Korzyn noticed, creating a distraction while I collected myself. He'd just lost his father, but he never held it against me, instead choosing to devote his life to protecting me.

We may not be brothers by blood, but we're brothers by choice.

And someone just attempted to murder him.

"What do we know?" My voice is rough, and I don't take my eyes off Korzyn's face as Rachiv steps closer to the bed.

My hand lingers near my sword, and I can feel his surprise as he pauses.

He clears his throat. "He was on his way to the marketplace, Your Majesty. The other human female slipped past her guards and had not returned."

The arm of the chair I'm sitting in cracks under my hand, and I realize I'm squeezing it.

Sarissa.

"Do you believe she is responsible for this?"

Rachiv sighs. "Korzyn does not trust her, but I find it difficult to believe she could take him unaware like this. His chest wound is high, making it an awkward strike for a female so much smaller."

I ignore that. After watching the way Vivian can shoot a crossbow, I'm sure I've misjudged the human females.

The human females I invited into my home.

"If this is true, she will regret it."

"Not...her."

I focus my attention back on Korzyn's face as his eyes open to slits. "What happened?"

"I was looking for her at the marketplace. A Zinta came out of nowhere and stabbed me."

"A Zinta?"

He nods. "I didn't recognize him. I was distracted or he wouldn't have succeeded." He looks disgusted with himself, and I attempt to hide my surprise. Never would I have imagined that Korzyn would allow himself to be distracted enough to almost be killed.

He lets out a pained chuckle at whatever he sees on my face. "She came back for me."

He groans at something the healer does, closing his eyes as she cleans his wound. He takes several deep breaths before his eyes open again.

"Sarissa. She pulled the cava berries from my pocket and put them in my mouth. Then she took my sword and guarded me, warning everyone to stay back. As soon as help arrived, she went after the Zinta." His eyes turn wild. "She's alone."

I turn to where Rachiv is standing with three of my most trusted guards. "Find her."

He nods, and Korzyn seems to relax slightly as they leave.

I watch Korzyn as his blinks get longer and longer. First, my uncle, and now the warrior who is as close to me as a brother. I clench my teeth so hard that my jaw begins to ache.

Korzyn opens his eyes again, and they're blurry with pain and exhaustion.

"Don't do anything hasty," he warns me. "Stick to the plan."

I growl at that but nod. Thanks to his spies, we know the traitors are planning to kill me at the ball. We've already discovered many of the guards who are working for my enemies. However, attempting to torture one for the information we need was useless. Whoever is in charge is smart enough to keep their identity hidden from those who could be used to betray them.

I sit with Korzyn all night. At one point, Vivian creeps in, handing me a plate of food. I almost refuse it, but the concern on her face makes me sigh and take a few bites.

"How's he doing?"

I shrug. "The healers say your cousin may have saved his life. If he hadn't eaten the cava berries when he did, he likely would have lost too much blood while the healers tried to get to him."

Vivian's face is pale, and I know she's worried about Sarissa.

"My guards will find your cousin."

She glances over her shoulder and then lowers her voice. "But what if they're the same guards who are allowing these attacks to happen?"

I take a deep breath, barely refraining from pointing out that she and her cousin are in league with those same guards.

We both look up at a knock on the door, and I take her wrist, dragging her behind me. No matter what this beautiful, conniving female does, it seems I'm unable to allow her to be in any danger.

"Your Majesty?"

It's Rachiv, and Bevix stands by his side, a grin on his face.

They part, and Vivian lets out a choked sob as they reveal Sarissa, her face pale, blood spattered across her dress.

"Oh my God. Are you—ewww!" Vivian gags, and I can't help but grin as Sarissa raises her hand, her long, delicate fingers wrapped around a Zinta's head.

Korzyn lets out a low laugh from behind me.

"Vicious female," he says, but his voice is appreciative.

Sarissa's face is hard. "He wouldn't tell me much. Said a guard named Inox passed on the message ordering the hit."

Bevix turns pale, while Rachiz curses. Behind me, I can practically hear Korzyn grinding his teeth. Inox is one of the few guards who have been with me since my father died.

No one can be trusted.

Vivian

I wander through the town, my shoes clicking on the cobblestones beneath my feet. The breeze smells of fresh flowers and baked bread, and the sun is shining, but my heart feels about as lively as a deflated balloon—and just as cheerful.

I mostly ignore the fact Cauri tied my dress too tight and it's cutting into my skin. Again.

I deserve all the pain in the world.

It's been three days since Korzyn was attacked, and he's already back on his feet. I'm guessing the cava berries were responsible for his quick recovery, but no one has ever told us anything about the berries or where they grow.

Which is probably for the best.

"Vivian!"

I glance over my shoulder, finding Sarissa striding toward me, ignoring the appreciative looks she's getting from men on both sides of the street. She's wearing a navy dress, her hair in a casual messy bun and her face determined. She looks like what she is—beautiful and dangerous.

"Hi," I mutter.

I can barely look at her, the chasm so deep between us that I don't know how to cross it.

She shifts on her feet. "I need to talk to you."

I shrug. "I'm listening."

"Not here."

I follow her to a small restaurant we've eaten in before. The smell of cooking meat is heavy in the air as we walk through the restaurant toward a corner where we won't be overheard. Two Zintas glare at her, thick eyebrows lowering as she passes by, and she sneers at them, her hand dancing over the hilt of the huge knife now hanging openly on her waist.

After what she did to the last Zinta that pissed her off, it's a good thing she's now making it clear she's armed.

A few Braxian women are seated next to a huge flower arrangement, and they wave to Sarissa, who nods back, a careless grin appearing on her face.

She waits until we're seated before that fake grin drops.

"I'm going to come right out and say it," she murmurs, glancing across the restaurant to where our guards have gotten their own table, several of them studying us carefully. "You were right, V, and I was wrong."

My mouth drops open. "Say that again."

The corner of her lips twitches before she lowers her voice even further, placing her elbows on the table as she leans close. The service here is notoriously terrible, with no menus to be found. Eventually, the owner will come around and dump a couple of bowls of stew on our table, ordering us to eat quickly so someone else can have our seats.

"At the market when Korzyn was attacked, it all became

clear. When I saw him lying there...no matter how much I hate him, I don't want him dead. We're in over our heads here. I overcompensated, I know I did. I always do."

Tears drip down my face at the despair in her voice. Sarissa feels like she has to save everyone because she thinks she failed to save Kelly. I can tell her it wasn't her fault until I'm blue in the face, but she'll never believe me. My cousin did everything she could that night—she has the scars to prove it.

"What are you saying?"

"I'm saying I thought I could betray these people, who've never done anything to hurt us. But I can't. You were right, you know. I'm broken. But I'm not a monster."

"I shouldn't have said that. I was upset because I couldn't face the thought of betraying Arix. You're right, it's more than just a fling. For me, anyway."

Sarissa sighs. "Well, I couldn't face the thought of telling the other women we don't have any way to get off Agron."

My stomach swims, Clara's words running through my head.

"We all have our stories. None of them are good. That's why I'm looking forward to getting off this planet. Maybe we'll be able to find a way to contact Earth. At the very least, we might be able to give our families some hope."

I push away the image of Clara's sad face for now. "They'll understand once we explain what happened. This isn't the end. We'll figure out a way to get that ship off Agron. I promise."

Sarissa nods, but I can tell she doesn't believe me.

"Do you want me to be the one to tell the others?"

She immediately shakes her head, her pale lips firming. "I can do it."

I reach out and squeeze her hand, relief hitting me like a drug.

"Okay," I say. "Now we just have to figure out how to get our hands on that chip without betraying the king."

Sarissa's face goes hard. "These assholes thought they could use our desperation? Let's make them see just how wrong they are."

Arix

Korzyn is back on his feet, no matter how many times I tell him to rest. "Our enemies wanted to kill me so you'd be vulnerable."

"Without Sarissa's quick thinking, they would have succeeded."

Korzyn's jaw tightens, and I almost laugh. He hates that he was taken by surprise. And he *loathes* being in debt to the little human.

Truthfully, I can't blame him.

Korzyn's gaze is steady on my face. "You have the chip now. Will you give it to them?"

I remove the tiny silver device from my pocket, holding it up, and we both watch as it gleams in the low light.

"Such a small thing to cause so much deception," I murmur. "I could snap it in the blink of an eye."

Korzyn shrugs dismissively. "You and I both understand the lengths a person will go to protect their family. And those human females consider one another to be family."

"I know." But the knowledge burns.

Korzyn is studying me, his silver eyes almost glowing,

and the hint of a smile plays around his mouth. "But you don't forgive her for it."

"The same qualities I admire about her, the ruthlessness, the deception, the commitment to her people...they are also the things that have allowed her to betray me."

"You would have done the same thing."

I nod. "I know. And the guilt wouldn't have eaten at me the way it eats at her. Some days, she can barely look at me. To guarantee my people's safety, I would do worse and never think twice."

"And yet."

I laugh humorlessly. "And yet."

"You're in love with her."

I shake my head, and Korzyn laughs.

"Why else would you allow her to take her deception this far while still sharing your bed?"

"I need our enemies to believe they have turned someone I trust."

"Tell yourself that as many times as you wish. But you could achieve the same by paying attention to her publicly and ignoring her in private. Unfortunately, you are unable to stay away from her."

His tone turns cutting, and I narrow my eyes.

"Careful."

"And there it is." He waves a hand, and I grind my teeth, but I've made it a habit to never lie to myself. Truthfully, Vivian *has* gotten under my skin.

But she doesn't have to stay there.

Tonight, I have a formal banquet with Mazark and some of our other allies from Kenritz, a large territory beyond my own kingdom. Thanks to my pact with Rakiz's tribe across the water and my ongoing alliances with those from this side of the water, I have grown my power to more than even my father could have dreamed.

Yet I feel hollow, dissatisfaction plaguing me with every step. I won't be seated near our guests for this banquet, and I find myself mourning the fact I won't get to see the expression on Vivian's face each time she tastes something new.

Focus on your kingdom. Soon she will leave Agron.

And I will be left here. Alone.

CHAPTER FOURTEEN

Vivian

"Do we have to go to this thing?" I mutter as Cauri arranges my hair into an updo that seems to need a thousand different tiny pins.

"Of course." She sniffs. "As the king's guests, it's your duty to attend."

I sigh. After my conversation with Sarissa, I have a feeling she's not going to make it tonight. Now that she knows Hesa—her maid—is working with Arix's enemies, she has banned her from her rooms after declaring she can get ready alone, much to Cauri's horror.

I've watched Cauri carefully since we learned Hesa was to be our contact to get messages to Varge. Cauri hasn't done anything to make me think she could be a traitor, and the way she adores the king makes it unlikely she's dirty.

But I'm being careful anyway.

Cauri leans down and opens a drawer, pulling out a

long, glimmering necklace. The jewels perfectly match my eyes, and I gasp as she fastens it around my neck, handing me matching earrings to fasten myself.

"The king asked you to wear these," she says.

I run one finger over the cool stones at my ears, my heart pitter-pattering at the thought.

I turn my head at a knock on the door, ignoring Cauri's scowl.

"Come in."

Sarissa pokes her head in the door. Like me, she's dressed only in a robe. Unlike me, her hair is out and falling down her shoulders, her face still completely free of any cosmetics.

"You're not getting ready?"

"I'm not going."

Cauri looks like she might have an aneurysm at this news, and I sigh.

"Can you give us a moment? Please?"

She sends Sarissa a dark look, muttering about selfish human females as she stalks out the door.

"What's going on?" I murmur, and Sarissa sits on the edge of my bed.

"I have a migraine."

"You don't get migraines."

"I know, but that's my cover story. I've been thinking about this situation, and I don't trust Varge. Unless he's an idiot, he won't be pinning all his hopes and dreams on us betraying Arix. I'm sure he and his merry band of traitors will have a backup plan. And if they do, they don't need us, which means we have targets on our backs."

My mouth goes dry, but I agree with her reasoning. "So what are we going to do?"

"You need to talk to Arix tonight and tell him everything.

I'm going to find Korzyn before dinner and do the same. Then I'm going to start putting our plan into motion."

My stomach turns to lead.

Maybe Arix will understand. Maybe he won't want to kick me out of his kingdom for conspiring against him.

I almost snort. Arix is as likely to bend as a steel beam, and just as likely to forgive.

I return my attention to Sarissa. "Are we going to have enough time?"

"We have to. I have enough contacts to get my messages out. But you need to be careful. Arix might lose his shit when you tell him everything."

My hands shake at the thought, but I bury them under my robe. "I'll be okay. Promise me you'll be careful too."

"I promise."

"Ahem." Cauri knocks on the door, and Sarissa sends me a look but pads out of my room, nodding at Cauri. Cauri frowns after her, and I sigh.

It's never good news for my scalp when Cauri is in a bad mood.

Arix

I place my crown on my head, staring into the mirror. My father was my age when he died, and I look almost identical to him.

Except for my eyes. I have my mother's eyes.

Although I never saw my mother's eyes look as cold as mine. Hers were always lit with joy or glowing with love. Two things I know little about.

My crown is one I don't wear often. The red jewels

contrast sharply with the black metal. The jewels were mined by one of my ancestors, and the crown's daintier twin sits alone in the vault that holds my mother's jewelry.

I glance across the room at where Korzyn is sitting next to the window, sharpening his sword. If I didn't see him lying in the healers' quarters, I would never know he is weaker than usual. His eyes are sharp, his face almost feral, as he stares into the distance.

"Your sources say we should expect an attack at the ball," I murmur, reaching for my own sword. It may be ceremonial, the handle covered in jewels, but I keep the blade sharp.

"Yes," Korzyn says. He glances over his shoulder at me, his jaw tightening. "But we would be smart to be wary each day leading up to the ball. Mazark has long wanted your territory for himself, and I find it difficult to believe his visit is coincidentally coinciding with your enemies' plans."

I nod, but my jaw hurts from grinding my teeth. "Do you ever wish we were normal males?"

Korzyn's gaze searches my face. "Normal?"

"Such as those Braxians from across the water."

"The barbarians? You believe they're normal?"

I give him a look, and he laughs, but his face quickly clears. "I don't know what I'd do with all my time if I weren't constantly fighting to stop you from being murdered, my friend."

"Well." I smirk. "Let's hope we get a chance to find out. Perhaps you can take up a hobby."

Korzyn raises his eyebrow, but he gets to his feet, striding toward the door. "I'm not the kind of male who does well with too much free time."

I snort. That is probably the truth. He would likely shift

all that unrelenting focus to a female, and that wouldn't be healthy for anyone.

I slide my sword into its scabbard and follow my adviser out the door. We walk in silence until we get to the huge banquet hall, and my gaze immediately find blue eyes that shine brighter than the Colossal Water on a sunny day. Vivian smiles at me, but it's hesitant, and my heart beats faster in my chest.

I allow my gaze to drink her in, from the top of the complicated hairstyle that reveals her smooth white neck, to the blue-green dress that perfectly matches her eyes, cupping her generous breasts.

She's wearing the jewels I gave her, and I have to fight to keep my body under my control at the sight.

Her smile widens as she runs her own gaze over my body, resting on the crown on top of my head. She raises her eyebrow, and I send her a wicked grin, stalking toward her table.

"Arix," Korzyn mutters, and I growl, forcing my attention away from the vixen at the far end of the long table to the large, bearded male who sits closer to the head, his eyes knowing as they watch me.

I nod at him, and the room goes silent as I stroll across the wide expanse of the room, noting the position of each of my guards—both those I can trust and those I can't.

As agreed, the ones who are most loyal to Korzyn are currently at the marketplace, rounding up those who collude against me as we speak. I take my seat, smiling to cover the rage that burns within me at the thought.

"Please," I say, waving my hand. "Eat."

Vivian

Arix looks like a dream, sitting at the head of the table. He's dressed from head to toe in unrelenting black. It matches his hair, contrasts with his skin, and allows the wild blue of his eyes to take center stage.

There will be dancing after this. I asked Cauri the difference between a banquet and a ball, and she looked horrified at my ignorance before explaining there will be no sit-down dinner at the ball and the focus will be more on the dancing, while tonight, the dancing is more like an afterthought.

I spoon up some kind of soup, enjoying the slight spiciness. I can feel eyes on me and glance up, finding Arix studying my face. The bearded man next to him follows his gaze, and I blush. He looks at me like I'm an insect he'd quite like to dissect, and I tear my eyes away from their table.

I don't know anyone here, and I make a little small talk with the friendly blue guy sitting next to me, who introduced himself as Nirix. But I mostly watch the king. He looks like he doesn't have a care in the world, but I know him well enough to see through that now. He's furious.

His eyes meet mine again, and I almost gasp at the rage burning within them. He glances at the man next to him, who has a smirk on his face as he murmurs something in a low voice.

"Who's that?" I ask Nirix when he pauses in his conversation with a Braxian woman. She sniffs and turns to the man on her other side, ignoring me, but Nirix leans close, careful not to impale me with the long horns sticking out of his head.

"That's Mazark. He rules the largest piece of Kenritz, a territory outside our kingdom. Next to him is Lirix, his second-in-command. According to rumors, Mazark's people are gradually beginning to prefer being ruled by Lirix."

"Why?"

He shrugs. "Mazark is cruel, and he hates Arix. He's unable to negotiate from a position of power—instead, he always resorts to threats. That means he has gradually lost more and more territory to Arix in exchange for his help in many of his wars."

This planet and its politics fascinate me. "I'm new on Agron," I murmur. "Will you tell me more?"

Nirix grins at me, displaying sharp teeth, and then throws back his drink, gesturing for a servant to bring him another one. He's already slurring slightly, but his loose tongue may be good news for me as he winks.

"Always happy to talk to a beautiful female," he says. "What do you want to know?"

"What else can you tell me?"

He grins again and sits back in his chair with a belch that doesn't go unnoticed by the Braxian female next to him. I hide my own grin as she turns up her nose and shifts her chair closer to the male sitting on her right.

"Okay," Nirix says. "On one side of the water, we have the barbarian tribes, ruled by tribe kings like Rakiz and Dexar. They negotiate for territory and make alliances based on threats to their people. On this side, we have a king who rules the largest territory, the Kingdom of Heriast. But he's increasingly alone and vulnerable as his enemies conspire against him." My heart clenches at that, but Nirix is clearly in his element. He pulls out a piece of paper, and I almost snatch it from his hands as I realize it's a rough map.

"Here," he says. "This area to the west is all wilderness, broken up by the many barbaric tribes across the Colossal Water. This here is the water, and to the East, you have Heriast. Southeast of that is Kenritz, which stretches over here until you hit the Prixor Forest."

"What's past the forest?"

He shrugs. "The forest is vast, and there are beasties in there that kill anything that enters."

Of course there are.

A servant tops up Nirix's cup, and a bell sounds.

"What's that?"

Nirix sighs, looking mournfully after the servant as she carries the noptri away. "Time for dancing."

Servants fling open the huge black doors on the right side of the banquet hall, and I follow the crowd into another room. It's huge, but according to Nirix, this isn't even half as large as the ballroom, which we'll be standing in within a few days.

I glance around. Gauzy white material drapes elegantly across the black walls, with huge metal chandeliers hanging above the smooth stone floor, which has been polished until it gleams. The air is redolent with the scent of flowers, while candles have been placed in the centers of small tables dotting the perimeter of the room, providing a place for guests to rest their feet.

Here and there, long, intricately designed scrolls are hanging on the walls—between the white material. They're covered in characters I can't read, and the fact they haven't been moved makes me think maybe they're important to either Arix or his people.

I glance around the room, wishing my cousin were here. With Arix busy, surely I can skip the rest of the night. I showed my face, so maybe now I can go find Sarissa.

I'm about to do just that when Nirix takes my hand, leading me onto the dance floor as music begins to play. The instruments sound completely different compared to those

I've heard on Earth, and I crane my neck, attempting to get a good look at them.

"I don't know these dances," I protest, and Nirix grins at me.

"I'll teach you."

I can feel hot eyes on me, but I avoid glancing around. Arix has more than enough to concentrate on, and Nirix doesn't mean me any harm. He's clearly already buzzed, but he shows me a few steps, twirling me in his arms as I deftly avoid colliding with his horns.

Within a few minutes, I'm out of breath, wishing Cauri had not once again tied my dress so tight. I laughingly pull away from Nirix, and he smiles, heading toward a servant who is circling the large room with cups of noptri.

Maybe now I can sneak away. I turn toward the door, bumping into a Braxian guard. He silently holds out a scroll, gesturing for me to take the paper. I reach for it, frowning. "What is it?"

He stalks away, and I shrug, wrinkling my nose as I realize it's damp.

I unravel it, and my hands shake as they're suddenly stained with red.

Bile fills my mouth. It's Sarissa's handwriting. I raise my head, searching for her in the crowd, but it's clear she's already been taken.

Just in case I needed more proof, a long lock of her blonde hair has been attached to the paper. Her writing is stark, and her fury is unmistakable.

DON'T GIVE THEM A FUCKING THING.

It's obvious this is supposed to be a ransom note. They've taken my cousin and made it clear they have her with the blood and the hair.

Only, they can't write in our language. They've assumed

my cousin would beg me to go through with our original plan—and betray Arix. But they don't know Sarissa at all.

Taking her hostage will just plain piss her off. Sarissa is cool under pressure and likely armed with weapons they won't expect. Unfortunately, she has a tendency to enrage people. She says it's because angry people make mistakes, but the thought of her infuriating her captors makes the hair on the back of my neck stand up. Angry people also kill their hostages.

My whole body goes numb as I move through the crowd, slamming into people as I frantically search for Korzyn. I'm cursing myself as my heart slams in my chest. I should've told Korzyn and Arix as soon as Sarissa and I were sure we weren't going to help the traitors.

Arix is suddenly in front of me, his hands on my face.

"I want to see you wearing nothing but those jewels," he murmurs, running one finger along the necklace.

I attempt a smile, conscious of the many eyes on us. Arix isn't fooled.

"What's wrong?" he asks, and I clamp down on my lower lip, fighting back the tears that attempt to spill down my cheeks.

"I need h-help," I admit. I glance around us, certain I'm being watched. "I need to tell you something."

Arix's face goes cold. "That you're planning my assassination? I already know."

CHAPTER FIFTEEN

V ivian

My mouth drops open, my breath strangled. "What?"

Arix frowns at me. "Every step you've taken has been closely watched since you arrived." He glances around us and smiles as if he doesn't have a care in the world. "Dry your tears, lovely. Now is not the time."

His voice is ice, and I can feel my heart breaking. He thinks I'd try to have him killed?

I shake myself. Of course he does. I haven't yet told him I've been playing both sides.

"We will step out," he says. "And you can tell me what's wrong." His voice is laconic, and I shake my head, but his hand is a hard clamp around my wrist.

I follow him numbly, my head spinning. "Wait, Arix," I say. He glances back, eyebrow raised, and I pull on my arm. "If they know I've told you—"

The room explodes.

Arix throws himself on top of me, and we roll beneath one of the tables, barely missing being crushed by a stone pillar as it smashes to the ground.

I cough. "Arix—"

"Fire!"

Screams begin, and I whirl, attempting to get up. Arix sighs, tucking me close. "How predictable."

"What the hell?"

He glances at me, but it's as if he doesn't even see me. Instead, he seems to be waiting. And it hits me.

"You've known about this the whole time."

He smiles, and there's nothing of the man I love in that smile. "People have been betraying me my entire life. Why should the beautiful female who held my heart in her tiny hand be any different?"

I blink at that, my mouth falling open, but Arix is already pushing me out the other side of the table, toward one of the long scrolls that hang on the walls.

"You don't understand," I cough. "I'm on your side."

Arix ignores me as he pushes the scroll aside and slams his hand on the wall, both of us choking as the air begins to fill with smoke. The wall swings open, and he pulls me through, pushing gently against my lower back.

He closes the wall behind us. "Run," he orders.

I can't see much. The passage is dimly lit, and I'm stumbling over my dress. Finally, I lean down and gather it in one hand, both of us sprinting down the hall.

"Where does this lead?"

We come to an intersection, and Arix lets out a low laugh, pulling me to the right. "Everywhere. My men are dealing with the traitors as we speak. Whoever is behind this won't be able to allow me to get away. You need to run toward the dock."

"What? I'm not leaving you!"

Arix ignores that, his hand clamped around mine as he encourages me to move faster.

Footsteps sound behind us, and the hair stands up on the back of my neck, terror making my knees weak.

"Of course you'd run into these passageways. So predictable. Sorry, Your Majesty, but there's no way out," a voice says, and Arix shoves me roughly behind him as a shadow appears in front of us.

"Bevix," Arix grinds out. "I must admit, I was expecting Rachiv."

Bevix smiles. "Rachiv is already dead," he says, and Arix's shoulders slump slightly. "We offered you every chance to hand over the throne. Now we'll take it from you. Just another accident in this cursed palace."

Arix snorts at that, looking completely unconcerned, and I almost roll my eyes. Trust him to face death with that "I don't give a fuck" look on his face.

"You were one of my father's closest advisers," Arix says, as if discussing the weather.

Bevix shrugs. "You lost the last shred of your support when you began negotiating with the barbarians across the water."

Arix smiles as screams echo down the corridor. "Those who *do* support me are currently killing each and every single one of your men. Traitors will never be tolerated in my court. It may have been necessary for me to take my time and appear defenseless and exposed while I discovered just who could be trusted, but you were never going to take my throne. Your numbers are much lower than you believe."

Bevix bares his teeth. Then he turns to me.

"Don't fret. There will be room in my bed for you. If

you're very good, perhaps I'll add a second throne next to mine."

"Fuck you."

He frowns. "We'll need to work on that mouth of yours. I suppose you don't really need a tongue, do you?"

If he's attempting to enrage Arix, it's not working. The king doesn't even look at me as Bevix draws his sword.

The castle shakes as something explodes, and Bevix's eyes widen.

I laugh. "You didn't think you were the only one who knew how to blow shit up, did you? That's the sound of Arix's subjects joining the fight. You see, they love him as their king. They don't want you. *No one wants you.*"

Arix glances at me, surprise in his eyes. No, I didn't tell him about this little plan. Sarissa and I scrambled to add to his ranks at the last minute. It turns out that of those who trade at the marketplace, most of his largest and strongest subjects much prefer him as king. And they were only too willing to help us. Somewhere out there, Dexar and his tribe have joined forces with Arix's men, leaving Rakiz's warriors to keep the main camp safe from the Dokhalls.

This fight needs to be wrapped up quickly, before the Dokhalls realize Rakiz's defenses have been split in half.

A roar reaches us, the sound so loud it seems to shake the castle, and I slam my hands over my ears.

"Oh, that?" I ask when it's finished. "That's Dragix. And you really shouldn't have fucked with the man who saved his life and helped his pregnant mate." I tsk. "Dragons are surprisingly loyal creatures."

Arix laughs, sending me an incredulous look, and I smile at him.

Bevix roars and lunges toward the king. Arix pushes me

against the stone wall and draws his sword, his face hard even as a tiny smile plays around his mouth.

Metal hits metal, and I wish I had a sword of my own. Not that it would help, since Arix and Bevix are moving almost too fast to see in the small space.

But I have my own knife. The one Zoey ensured was coated in poison before she handed it to me. It's currently tucked into a thigh sheath Nevada insisted I take.

I just need to get close enough to use it.

Bevix swings wildly, losing patience, and Arix steps smoothly away, laughing as his adviser's sword hits the rocky wall.

From the way he flashes his teeth, Arix has been waiting for this moment for a long time.

A scuffle sounds behind me, and I turn, raising my hands to defend myself, but it's too late.

"Zion?"

He shoves his sword deep into my stomach, his grin fierce. My scream merges with Arix's roar, and I slump to my knees.

He's one of the guards Arix trusted with my safety.

I blink, and Arix is suddenly there. I blink again, and Zion's head is no longer on his body. Another blink, and I'm lying on my back, Arix leaning over me.

I manage to push him away. "Behind...you."

Arix spins, his sword once again meeting Bevix's. The adviser's face is pale, and his clothes are red in places as he bleeds from small cuts and slashes.

Arix has been toying with him like a cat with a mouse. But he's no longer playing with him now.

In fact, he's barely paying attention, his eyes wild as they meet mine.

"Hold on," he orders me. "Just hold on."

Agony engulfs my entire body. I thought I knew what pain was when I shoved Nevada aside, taking a sword to the chest.

That was nothing compared to this.

My entire abdomen burns as if it's aflame. I writhe uncontrollably, small noises leaving my throat. Death would be a blessing right now.

Arix is getting sloppy, most of his attention on me. This is exactly what Bevix planned for. He knew he'd never take down the king who trains every morning as if possessed. So he decided to kill me first, splitting Arix's focus so he could take his head.

Not if I can help it.

I reach my hand down and almost pass out as the pain feels like a hundred knives, all of them buried deep in my gut.

I always wanted to be more than decoration. Now I get to save the life of a king on an alien planet.

Look at me now, Mom.

My mind is wandering, and I ruthlessly force myself to focus. Just a little longer, and then I can close my eyes.

Arix moves closer to me, and Bevix laughs, batting Arix's sword away and stabbing his own sword into Arix's chest.

No. Please no.

I scream, attempting to get up, but I'm too weak, my blood pooling around me. I must be dreaming, because Arix doesn't die. Instead, he laughs, slashing his sword down Bevix's arm while the other male curses.

It takes a while for my foggy brain to understand. Then Arix's shirt parts, revealing a glimmering emerald green, which darkens to black.

Dragon scales. Arix is wearing dragon scales beneath his shirt.

Bevix lets out a strangled sound, and this time, he's the one getting sloppy as fury makes him swing wildly. But Arix is barely paying attention as he attempts to get closer to me.

"Stay awake," he roars, and I nod. I'm not finished yet.

My hand inches down. Thankfully, my dress has a long slit, and I'm sprawled on the ground, the knife strapped to my thigh, taunting me with how close it is.

I wrap my hand around the knife, but I can't pull it free of Nevada's thigh sheath. I tug, but nothing happens. Frustration makes my heart pound, and I force myself to relax. A pounding heart means even more blood will be pouring out of my body.

The ringing in my ears and the black spots taking over my vision tell me I'm losing consciousness. My mouth falls open as Nevada's face appears in front of my eyes, her teeth bared. "Fight," she orders me, and Ellie nods from where she stands next to her, tears streaming down her cheeks.

"You've got this, Viv."

Zoey is suddenly there too. "Just get it in his bloodstream like we talked about," she urges. "He'll weaken instantly, I promise."

My eyes want to close, but Charlie scowls at me. "Wake up," she commands.

Ivy nods in agreement. "Make him hurt, V."

I try again, a sob leaving me as my hand slips off the knife. I can't get it free.

"Based on that asshole's current trajectory, he will be in front of you in approximately twenty seconds," Alexis points out, and I grind my teeth.

"Nineteen, eighteen, seventeen." It's Beth, counting down, her voice musical.

"Pull out the knife, V." Sarissa's voice keeps me conscious

as I scream a curse, using what feels like every last ounce of my strength to wiggle the knife free.

Sarissa smiles proudly at me, and the women all disappear as I blink again.

Blood loss. I'm either close to death or I'm going insane.

I shake it off, and the rest of the world fades away as I turn my head, waiting until Bevix dances just close enough.

He doesn't see me as a threat. No one ever sees me as a threat.

He won't make that mistake again.

My hand whips out, and my knife slashes across his ankle, drawing blood. He curses, stomping his boot onto my hand.

I scream, but so does he.

Zoey promised me the poison would be fast-acting, and she was right. Bevix leans down and claws at his foot, then he throws his head back, another scream leaving his throat.

He raises his sword, turning toward me, and I switch the knife to my other hand as he advances on me, the rage in his eyes making it clear he's got nothing left to lose.

I throw the knife, savage pleasure filling me as the blade buries itself in his throat. Bevix makes a choking sound and falls to his knees.

"Hey, look, my party trick had a purpose after all."

Arix slams his sword into Bevix's chest and then kicks the other male away, leaving him to bleed out.

The way I'm bleeding out.

Arix pulls me into his arms, and I cough, a metallic taste in my mouth. That can't be good.

"For what it's worth," I manage to get out, "we were never going to allow you to be hurt."

Anguish flashes through his eyes, although it's quickly replaced by the steely determination I know so well.

"I know. Be quiet and conserve your strength."

I laugh at that but quickly stop when it makes the pain worse.

I reach for Arix's hand and squeeze. "Listen to me. Please."

It's the "please" that does it. He leans down, pressing his forehead against mine.

I take a deep breath, needing to get this out. "My whole life, I'd thought my only worth was in my looks. And beauty is fleeting, which meant I had to hold on to that beauty as tightly as I could, for as long as I could. I thought no one would truly want me. I thought I was unlovable."

Tears are streaming down my face, and Arix moves back slightly so he can brush them away, his midnight eyes dark with sorrow.

I force a smile. "So I pushed people away first. I was willing to betray you at first because I knew you were never going to be able to love me for me anyway. So I might as well use you to help us all get off this planet."

I can hear footsteps running toward us, and I know I don't have much time. It's getting harder and harder to speak.

"Except you're a good man. An incredible ruler who cares about his people. And when I'm with you, you make me feel like...*more*. I'm not just the girl who's only good for posing in front of a camera. With you, I feel smart. I feel funny. I feel *seen*."

He brushes his mouth against mine, the movement gentle.

"So thank you, Arix. And I'm sorry. I never would've let them hurt you. I hope you know that now."

I force another smile, but he doesn't smile back, his expression a picture of grief.

"Don't you dare give up," he says through his teeth, glaring down at me. "You belong to me."

Tears fill my eyes at the words I've always wanted to hear. They're bittersweet. Why is life so unfair?

"Will you hold me? I'm so cold."

Arix's enraged roar is the last thing I hear as my eyes slide shut.

CHAPTER SIXTEEN

A rix

"Why hasn't she woken up yet?" I demand, almost unable to look at the human female who is lying so still in my bed.

The healer gives me a sympathetic look. But she doesn't lie to me. Her honesty is the reason she is the healer I trust with my own health.

"She may not wake, Your Majesty. Humans are much smaller than Braxians, and their bodies are much less efficient at replacing their own blood. Severe blood loss can lead to brain damage and organ failure."

"She was talking before she lost consciousness." I don't mention that she seemed to be mumbling to her human friends, who were obviously nowhere near the tunnels where we were.

The healer sighs. "The cava berries can only do so much. Even Dragix said his healing may not work due to the amount of blood she lost. For now, you must bargain with the gods."

That I can do.

Fury makes my hands shake as I stare down at Vivian's face, so pale against the dark blankets.

Korzyn's paranoia once again proved to save us. The healer had alerted him that Bevix's men had set fire to our cava berries—obviously to ensure our deaths. But hadn't counted on Korzyn, who secretly—and illegally—harvested berries of his own a few months ago. They're currently growing close to my mother's garden.

"Why isn't she waking up?"

I turn at Sarissa's voice as she pushes open the door. Her face is pale with grief, and her arm is covered in bandages. She refused any cava berries when Korzyn found her lost in the forest after she'd killed her captor and freed herself. She insisted the berries go to those who had more serious injuries, curling her lip at Korzyn when he threatened to shove them down her throat.

I glance at my commander, whose gaze is fixated on the bandages wrapped around Sarissa's arm, his eyes hard. I send him a look, and he returns his attention out the window, although I have no doubt that his entire focus is still on the female who is currently holding back tears.

"The healer said her brain may have been damaged," I mutter.

Sarissa lets out a choked sob, and I can practically feel Korzyn's rage as he slowly turns his head in my direction, likely unhappy with my brutal honesty. I ignore him, stepping closer to Vivian and taking her cool hand in mine.

"She has to wake up," Sarissa says, firming her lips. She brushes her tears off her face and leans close to her cousin.

"Enough with the dramatics, V. It's time to rejoin the land of the living. We need you."

We all watch Vivian intently for a moment, but she gives no indication she has heard us. Her eyes don't flutter; her fingers don't twitch. I press a kiss to her hand before gently laying it back down on the bed.

"I need to go talk to Dexar," I say, and Sarissa nods.

"I'll stay with her."

She's careful to keep her gaze away from Korzyn, who silently follows me from the room.

"I had them brought to your quarters," Korzyn says. "I know you don't want to leave her."

I nod and push open the door, finding Dexar and Alexis —his queen. Dragix also leans against the wall, his arm wrapped around his mate's waist. From the look on his face, he's not at all happy she insisted on coming with him.

"How is she doing?" Alexis demands. "The others wanted to be here, but Rakiz thought it best if we left camp in smaller numbers to keep from drawing the Dokhalls' attention."

My throat tightens, and I can't say the words. Korzyn glances at me, his eyes sympathetic, before he returns his gaze to Alexis.

"The same," he says.

Charlie's hand shakes as she pushes her hair off her face, while Alexis's lips tremble until she presses them together, turning and burying her head against Dexar's chest.

I have to turn away from the sight, moving toward the window. My lovely female thought she had no one but her cousin. Thought she had no true family. The anguish these females are showing proves differently.

She once told me Rakiz's tribe was a family. But the words were wistful, as if she was not part of that family.

Wake up, Vivian, and see how much these people care for you.

Charlie takes a deep breath. "Can we see her?"

I nod, and the females immediately move into my bedroom, where *my* female still lies as if dead, five days after one of my guards stabbed her with the sword I gave him.

I didn't even think to make her wear dragon scales. Didn't believe she could be targeted. Her struggle to stay alive is my fault.

Korzyn glances at me again and obviously realizes I'm incapable of anything that doesn't involve sitting by Vivian's side and begging her to wake up.

"We thank you for your help," Korzyn says formally, and both males nod.

"Rakiz would have come, but he refuses to leave his mate while his child is so young," Dexar murmurs, and I nod.

The first time I saw this male, I mocked him, calling him a barbarian. And yet it was his forces that secured my castle while I was unable to leave Vivian's side.

"All your current guards have been interrogated," Dragix says, his eyes hooded as he leans against the wall.

"Explain," I say, and his eyes flash gold. "Please," I amend, and he shows me his teeth but complies.

"I am able to speak mind to mind." I gape at him as his voice sounds in my head, his lips clamped shut.

"I had thought you were only able to speak this way to your female," I admit.

"I usually choose only to speak to my Charlie this way," he says, glancing toward my bedroom as if already missing his mate. I attempt to suppress the jealousy that crawls down my throat, making it impossible to talk.

Wake up, Vivian. I need you.

"With a few words in their minds, Dragix was able to

convince your men he can read their thoughts." Dexar smiles, flashing white teeth. "A brilliant idea, really. Three guards confessed instantly, while a fourth was later found to be aware of the traitors, even if he wasn't colluding directly with them."

"Thank you," I say, itching to return to Vivian. "I will need a few days to get my army in order, and then we will march toward Rakiz's camp."

Dexar frowns, and Korzyn clears his throat.

"We will join your war against the Dokhalls," he says.

While we had agreed to provide warriors for their fight, today marks the first day of our official alliance with the barbarian tribes.

Dragix shows no surprise, but I can practically feel it radiating off the dragon.

"Why?"

"You came to my aid with nothing to gain," I say.

"The human females are under our protection," Dexar reminds me.

"You could easily have had them smuggled out," Korzyn says. The hint of a smile plays around his mouth. "They would have fought like wild karja, but I believe you could have taken them back across the water."

"Vivian and Sarissa asked for our help."

I turn away, unable to speak when it feels as if a mishua is standing on my chest. While I had thought my female was conspiring against me, she was secretly planning to use her contacts to save me and anyone loyal to me.

"And you provided that help," Korzyn says. "It will be remembered."

My hands itch with the need to return to my bedroom, and I glance over my shoulder.

Dragix's voice interrupts my thoughts.

"We will take our females home now. Be prepared though; they have already set up a schedule for visits. I will be flying back with Beth and Ivy in the morning."

Dragix's eyes lighten in amusement, and I nod. I don't believe I will ever get used to hearing another voice in my head.

Alexis and Charlie return, both of them with reddened eyes. Their males instantly engulf them in their arms, and I can no longer stand to watch. I nod to them and turn, stalking back into my room, where Vivian is still unconscious, her face too pale.

Sarissa gets up from the bed and walks out, her movements slow, as if each step is difficult. Korzyn murmurs something to her in the next room, and her voice is hoarse as she replies.

I lie down on my side next to Vivian, ignoring the healer as she walks away, muttering something about returning later to change Vivian's bandages.

"This is the second time you have almost died on my planet," I murmur, stroking Vivian's hair off her face. "Not counting the way you crashed here on that ship. When you wake up, you'll need to convince me not to tie you to my bed, where I can keep you safe."

I lay my head on her pillow, breathing her in. "You will wrinkle your nose and give me that disdainful look, and I will fantasize about pulling off your clothes. Then you'll say something sarcastic, and I'll kiss your smart mouth."

I nuzzle her cheek, attempting not to notice how cool her skin is. I pull more blankets over her, making a mental note to add more logs to the fire.

"I'm lonely without you," I murmur against her skin. "I need you."

This is my fault. I was so focused on avenging my

parents that I failed to protect the female who means every-thing to me. I tried my best to push her away, to treat her as if she was just another female warming my bed. But the moment I watched Zion slide his sword into her stomach was the moment I ceased lying to myself.

Vivian is mine. And when she wakes up, I'll make her realize I'm hers too.

I sigh, my throat raw with barely suppressed rage. My enemies succeeded after all. They may not have killed me, but they've broken me into pieces.

Vivian

My stomach is burning me alive.

I wince, shifting in an attempt to alleviate the pain, but it only gets worse.

Something tightens around my chest, and my breath comes in sharp pants.

"Vivian? Open your eyes."

Eyes. That's right. I have eyes. But they're so heavy. Maybe if I keep them closed for a little longer, the pain that's clawing its way through my body will disappear.

"Please, lovely. It's been eight days."

My brow furrows, and even that slight movement seems to excite the low voice in my ear.

"Eight days without those beautiful blue eyes staring into mine. Have mercy, Vivian. Show me you're still with me."

The voice is hoarse and...tormented. It's full of pain and sorrow, and for some reason, it makes my chest hurt worse.

I'll do anything to take the pain from that voice.

Opening my eyes feels like tunneling through concrete, but I take a deep breath, ignoring the way it pulls at my stomach.

"There you are."

I blink as I stare up at the most gorgeous face I've ever seen.

"She may be groggy," a feminine voice says. "We also don't know if the blood loss has damaged her brain."

That face tenses as the man bares his teeth in the direction of that voice, and footsteps sound, followed by the opening and closing of a door.

"You know who I am, don't you, lovely?"

Arix. It all comes back to me now. My stomach hurts because I was fucking impaled on Zion's sword.

Arix looks like he's aged twenty years. He has new lines between his brows, and from the dark circles under his eyes, he hasn't slept properly for days.

I shift, immediately wincing at the pain, and Arix turns, roaring for the healer to return.

"That depends," I manage to get out, and every word feels like an achievement. "How pissed are you at me?"

I don't think I've ever seen relief take over someone's face the way it does Arix's. His expression goes blank, and then he closes his eyes, burying his head against my neck as he shudders.

Someone clears their throat, and he pulls away, leaving me mourning the loss of him. He doesn't go far though, taking a cup from one of his healers.

"This will help with the pain," she says.

"Will it make me sleepy?"

I'm tired of sleeping. Eight days is a lot to miss out on.

She nods, and I frown, opening my mouth, but Arix brings it to my lips, his eyes hard.

"Please," he says. "It...hurts me to see you in pain."

The guy knows just what to say to make me fall in line, and I sigh, sipping at the liquid. It tastes fruity, with an underlying bitterness, but it hits quickly. I don't appreciate the feeling of floating above my body, but the pain from my abdomen is no longer roaring through me like a wildfire.

"We need to talk," I mumble.

"When you're feeling better."

I open my mouth to protest, but Arix lies next to me, gently pulling me close, and I sigh instead, soaking in the feel of him against me.

Even if it is just temporary.

CHAPTER SEVENTEEN

V ivian

"Arix, come on. If I don't get out of this bed soon, I'm going to go crazy."

"You're still injured."

"The healers said I'm okay to start moving around."

"They said you could go to the bathing room by yourself. They said nothing about roaming the castle."

Stubborn male. I scowl at him, and he frowns right back before returning his attention to the papers he's reading.

He hasn't had me moved back to my rooms. Instead, he's working from the long sofa in front of the fire, where he can make sure I'm not doing anything crazy like, you know, walking to his sitting room without help.

"Give it a rest, cuz. You know he's not going to let you out of bed until the healers give you the all-clear."

I frown at Sarissa, who grins at me, raising one eyebrow.

"To be fair, after what happened, you can't really blame

him. I heard it was all very dramatic. Lots of killing and fainting. Very Romeo and Juliet of you."

Sarissa has lost weight, her cheekbones sharper than ever. Guilt swims through me at the reminder of what my near death did to my cousin. She's already lost more than most people. Watching me come so close to checking out must have been hell for her.

Apparently, Varge quickly knew we weren't going to cooperate. So the traitors' plans had to change. Step one was to take out Sarissa so she couldn't talk about what she had seen. Then Bevix would keep me hidden away in his rooms until he was bored with me and have me killed too. They'd tell Rakiz we'd both been killed during the assassination, and he'd never know differently.

Except they obviously don't know Rakiz or Nevada, because they would have showed up with the largest army they could find. Then they would've opened up a can of whoop-ass.

I lift my arm, reaching for a cup of water, and wince. Truthfully, I still feel like shit. The healers hover around me constantly, and they seem as surprised as I am that I'm not dead.

I got lucky when Zion stabbed me. He missed my critical organs, but I still lost a crazy amount of blood. The cava berries helped my body regenerate that blood, but it's left me weak as a kitten.

"Helloooo," a voice calls. Arix glances at me and sighs, and I can't help but laugh.

"I told you to let me go back to my rooms."

He shakes his head, his gaze running over my body possessively. "You're right where I want you."

"Ick," Sarissa says, and I smirk at her. Something relaxes in my chest when Arix gets all growly and makes it clear he still wants me. He refuses to talk about what happened, saying it can wait until I feel better. Truthfully, I'd rather get that conversation over with. I don't want him to feel forced to keep me here because I'm still recovering. If he's going to kick me and my cousin out of his kingdom, I'd rather he do it before I get even more attached.

Sarissa glances down at the notes she's writing, her brow furrowing. Obviously, we had no chance to find the control chip we need. Now Sarissa is frantically attempting to figure out a solution to our problem before we have to tell Clara and the others there's no chip.

"You're still in bed?" Nevada grins at me, Rakiz by her side. Arix nods at him, getting to his feet, and with a final glance at me, he gestures for the tribe king to follow him into the sitting room.

I poke my tongue out at her. "Apparently, I'm a fragile flower."

"You almost died." Sarissa's voice is sharp, and Nevada raises her eyebrow.

"Here," she says, handing Danica to her. "Take a chill pill."

Ivy follows Nevada into the room, closing the door behind her. "You can't just dump your baby on everyone," she tells Nevada.

"Wait, I can't?"

Sarissa rolls her eyes, but even she isn't immune to the cuteness overload that is Danica, and she grins down at her, making cooing sounds. "How is she so big already?"

"I know, right?" Nevada smiles. "She's growing like a weed."

"How'd she like her first flight?"

"She loved it. She'll have Uncle Dragix doing barrel rolls

with her as soon as she's talking. Dani has that dragon wrapped around her little finger."

She plops down on the bed, while Ivy moves closer to Sarissa, blowing a raspberry at Danica.

"Charlie couldn't make it today. She's sick again."

I frown. "What about that berry tea?"

"She's used it all," Ivy says. "Now that supplies of the cava berries are even more limited, she forbade Dragix from asking for more."

"I'm sure he took that well," Sarissa says, gently bouncing Danica in her arms.

Nevada rolls her eyes. "You know those Braxians. He'd be fine with someone else losing a leg or two as long as Charlie could keep her breakfast down."

I laugh. "They are rather single-minded. You guys don't need to come every day, you know."

The other women have been taking turns. Beth and Zoey visited yesterday, Zoey leaving behind a salve for my scar. Truthfully, I look forward to each visit, not just because they're good distractions from the beautiful man watching me from his sofa.

Nevada waves her hand. "You nearly died, dummy. Besides, we use the opportunity to keep an eye out for Dokhalls. Turns out, they're finding it difficult to recruit Zintas after Arix made it clear anyone caught helping them would be thrown out of his kingdom."

My heart warms at that, but I scowl in frustration.

"And how's your Braxian?" Nevada asks. "I notice you're still in his bed."

I chew on my lip, ignoring Sarissa's laugh. "We haven't talked yet."

Ivy lets out a low whistle. "Wish I could be a fly on the wall for that conversation. It's going to be a doozy."

I glower at her, but I can't help but smile as she grins at me, her eyes sparkling with fun. "I'm glad I can be entertaining."

"Someone has to be. We're all locked up in that camp with nothing to do but gather our armies. Vrex has his spies, but he's too recognizable to get intel himself. He's going out of his mind with boredom."

We chat for a few more minutes, but my eyelids are soon so heavy I can barely keep them open.

"We'll let you get some rest." Ivy smiles while Sarissa hands Danica back to Nevada. I'm still too weak to hold her, so Nevada leans down close to the bed so I can press a kiss against the baby's soft head.

"Thanks for visiting."

"Anytime."

With a final wave, they're gone in a whirlwind of sarcasm and quick grins.

"Those women could run this planet," Sarissa murmurs, and I laugh as my eyes slide closed.

Vivian

Today's the day.

I've finally been given the all-clear to resume my normal activities.

If those activities include spending most of the day resting.

Whatever. I'm no longer bedbound, and that's all that matters. Because that means Arix finally has to talk to me.

"You said we could talk when I was better. I'm better."

"You're still weak."

We're standing in his sitting room, a large tray of what's supposed to be our lunch sitting on the table between us.

"Do you want me to leave? Is that why you won't have this conversation with me until I'm completely better?"

Arix scowls. "No."

I walk back into his bedroom, picking up the long piece of paper I've been keeping beneath my pillow. Arix follows me, his eyes dark and unfathomable.

"I have something for you," I say.

He raises one eyebrow, but his gaze drops to the long scroll in my hand. "What is it?"

"A list of everyone who betrayed you," I say around the lump in my throat. "I guess my name should be at the top of the list, but you already know about me. Your advisers and guards weren't as careful as they should've been around me and Sarissa. We investigated the man who made the deal with us, and we were able to tie him to a few people in this castle. I know Dragix did some digging of his own, but I thought you could cross-check what you already know against this list."

I hand him the scroll and clasp my empty hands together. "We hadn't realized all roads led to Bevix, obviously, but these are the people we know for sure were in on the plan to take your crown."

"And my head."

I flinch. "And your head."

My heart thunders as his eyes meet mine, but for the first time in a long time, I can't determine what he's thinking.

"Don't blame yourself," he finally says. "Your guards were expected to allow you to be approached in that market."

I'd thought it was Zion who made that happen. I frown. "You set me up? You son of a bitch."

He laughs. "Need I remind you that you were actively betraying me this entire time?"

"I didn't think you'd get hurt, you jackass. And I couldn't go through with it in the end. You knew someone would use me?"

"I figured it was likely. Neither you nor your cousin was subtle about how badly you want to get off this planet." His mouth twists, and I lift my chin, my nostrils flaring. His words run through my mind, and for a moment, I'm back in that room, his hard body covering mine, protecting me from the explosions.

"People have been betraying me my entire life. Why should the beautiful female who held my heart in her tiny hand be any different?"

I clear my throat. "You thought I'd set you up to be assassinated."

He shrugs. "It seemed likely, based on what I knew of my enemies. But Varge cracked under torture. He told Korzyn about how the original plan was to assassinate me at the ball. It wasn't until they realized you and Sarissa couldn't be trusted to fulfill your part of the deal that they moved their plans up to the banquet."

"And the dragon scale?"

"Insurance. A good way to see who the traitor was. My only regret is I didn't anticipate them hurting you. If I'd been thinking clearly, I would've made sure you were wearing a scale too."

"I thought you were dead when he thrust that sword at you." He shrugs, and I scowl. "What if he aimed for your head?"

"Either way, it would have been over. I refuse to live my

life surrounded by people I can't trust. I'd rather choose death."

I glance away at that. Of course honor would mean everything to a man who lost his parents to the worst betrayal imaginable.

My head is suddenly spinning, and I sink into the closest chair. Arix is instantly kneeling in front of me, his hands cupping my face.

"Are you okay? Do you need a healer?"

"I'm fine. Just dealing with the fact you knew this whole time. Was anything between us real?"

I expect him to smile and make a lewd joke about the numerous times he took me to bed over the past few weeks. Instead, disappointment flashes in his eyes, quickly covered by indifference as he gets to his feet.

"I have something for you too."

He reaches into his pocket and then holds up his hand. I frown, getting to my feet, and it's not until he angles his hand closer to the light that I realize he's holding something tiny between his finger and his thumb.

I lower my head. It looks like a...chip.

I glance up, meeting his midnight gaze. "I don't understand."

"I've had my people searching for it ever since I declared war on the Dokhalls. It was surprisingly easy to get them to turn on each other with a little torture. Within days, we knew which group of Dokhalls had the chip. My warriors were instructed to carefully search every Dokhall they killed."

I stare at him, my heart racing. We can get off this planet. We can get revenge. If we want, we can even get back to Earth—back to our lives. So why do I feel like crying?

Arix is studying my face intently. Whatever he sees has brought a faint smile to his face.

"What are you thinking?" he asks me.

"I-I don't know," I stutter. "Th-thank you. You didn't need to do this."

"This is what you want. For some reason, I've been consumed with giving you what you want from the moment I've met you." He glances away. "To my own detriment."

Guilt twists my heart. "I'm sorry."

"I know."

"Will you forgive me?"

"That depends."

I blink at him. "On what?"

He gives me an enigmatic look but doesn't reply, and I scowl at him.

He just shakes his head. "You should give this to your cousin," he says, placing the chip in my hand and wrapping my fingers securely around it. He kisses my fist and then walks away, ignoring me as I call his name.

Sarissa is in her room, once again scanning her notes. She glances up, her mouth curling.

"Good to see you back on your feet. Are you hungry?"

I can't even speak, so instead, I hold up the chip. Sarissa's mouth falls open, and she jumps to her feet, snatching it from my hand, her fingers handling it as if it's made of glass.

"What. The. Fuck."

"Arix had his people looking for it this whole time." My lower lip trembles, and I clamp my teeth down on it.

"Wow. You must be incredible in bed. Good work, cuz."

She grins at me, but I can't even bring myself to fake a smile.

"What's wrong?"

I can't speak around the lump in my throat, and she tilts her head.

"V," she says. "This is incredible. This means we can probably get off this planet. We're going to make the Grivath pay for what they did to us. And the Dokhalls too. No other human women are going to go through what we went through."

I nod, and she stares at me for a long moment, finally stepping away and throwing up her hands.

"It's the royal cock, isn't it?"

I nod, blinking back tears. "Not just the cock but the man himself. I don't think I can leave him."

She sighs. "What did I tell you, Viv? Don't get attached. What happens if we get off this planet and leave you behind and then you guys break up or something?"

My heart sinks at the thought. "I must be an idiot because it's a risk I'm willing to take."

Sarissa sighs. "You're not an idiot. You're in love."

I stare at her. "Wait. Were you testing me just now?"

She laughs, but her eyes are wet. "You're willing to give up any future that includes Starbucks. That says it all."

I turn to pace. I *am* in love.

I thought I knew what love was. I believed it was like an ember, hidden and protected deep within a person's soul. In reality, love is a wildfire that burns away everything you thought you knew. It creeps up on you, almost silent, until you're suddenly overcome, surrounded by flames. And you'd run right through those flames if it meant you could spend the rest of your life with that person.

But life isn't a fairy tale.

"What if I stay, and then in a few months, we're tired of each other?"

"After what you guys went through, I'm willing to bet

that won't happen. He loves you, girl. As much as I'd like to tell you otherwise, so you'd come with me, it's obvious every time you're in the same room together. Sometimes, he stares at you like it'd physically hurt him to look away. And every now and then, his hands curl, as if he wants to reach for you and he's barely holding himself back."

I stop pacing and stare at her, my heart racing. "Are you serious?"

She gives me a look. "Trained observer, remember? I know what I've seen. Not to mention, he was an absolute mess when you were unconscious for all those days. Korzyn had to threaten to drug him to get him to eat and bathe."

I chew on that, turning to look out the window at the gardens below. "Do you think I'd be making a mistake if I stayed?"

"I don't want you to stay, but that's my selfishness. I feel like I just found you, and I don't want to lose you again. But you have to do what's best for you. Love like yours...I think you're lucky if it happens once in a lifetime. You'd be a fool to turn your back on it."

"So what do I do now?"

"Sounds like you need to go talk to that arrogant king. And I need to figure out how to get this chip back to Alexis."

I open my mouth to protest, but she points toward the door, her eyes sparkling. "Go."

I go.

I don't yet have the energy to run, but I walk as fast as I can down the hall. Urgency fills me, and I curse my puny body as I make my way back toward Arix's rooms.

My breath leaves me as I slam into a chest, falling backward. Strong arms grab me, barely preventing me from landing on my butt.

Arix.

His face is tormented.

"Running already?"

I open my mouth, and he gives me a slight shake.

"The moment I saw you, I knew you'd ruin me."

I blink at him, still winded, and he pulls me closer, leaning down until his face is close to mine.

"You're a liar," he growls. "You're wild, and you don't even know it. You deceive when it suits you, even if you may feel bad about it. You'll do anything to get your way if you can justify it as saving someone else. Even if it means you'll never be happy."

I open my mouth, and he leans even closer with a snarl.

"And I love you unreservedly. It makes me stupid. You've managed to bring a king to his knees. So will you leave me here, crawling for you? Or will you admit you love me back?"

His words loosen something tight in my chest, and suddenly I can take a full breath again. I raise my hand, burying it in his hair. His expression turns feral, and I bare my teeth at him, furious, ecstatic, and completely, incredibly alive.

"I love you," I snarl. "So much that it hurts. Are you happy now?"

He throws his head back and laughs. "Happy?"

He bends his knees, and I'm suddenly in his arms as he stalks back toward his rooms.

"I was waiting for you before I knew you existed," he murmurs, and I lean up, winding my arms around his neck.

"You truly love me?"

"I would let no other female even think about betraying me. I imagined it was just the way we tumbled, or perhaps the thrill of someone new. But when I thought you'd never wake up, I wanted to lie down next to you and not move for the rest of my life."

He pushes open the door to his rooms, and I wipe my wet face against his shirt. He lets out a low laugh. "No more of that."

My tears continue to fall, and he gently places me on the ground before kissing the tears from my face.

I sniff. "I always thought I was the fuckup. I thought I'd never amount to anything, so I never tried to be more than they said I could be. I sat and let them take photos of me, and I smiled, and I moved my arms and my legs and tilted my head, and I grew up and did it all again. And then I came here. And you taught me I was more than a puppet."

"Shh," Arix soothes me. "You are many things, but you're no one's puppet."

I give him a shaky smile, and he cups my face with his huge hand, leaning down to brush his lips against mine. The kiss is slow, gentle, and so tender that tears fill my eyes once more.

My stomach flutters at the feel of his hands on me. It seems like it's been years since he touched me like this, and I moan, pulling him closer.

He refuses to deepen our kiss, and I let out a growl that makes him chuckle against my mouth.

"More," I demand.

"Shh. Gently."

He keeps his mouth on mine as he lifts me, carrying me to the bed, where he follows me down until I'm lying on my back and he's leaning over me.

My hands clutch at his shoulders, and then I'm attempting to pull off his shirt as he lets out a slightly strangled laugh.

"No, lovely. You're not yet healed enough for that."

I growl. "Are you kidding me?"

"Let me make you feel good."

I open my mouth to give him explicit instructions detailing exactly how he can do that, but he shuts me up with another kiss, his hands moving to the ties on my dress. He loosens them, letting out a low groan as my breasts pop free.

Within moments, I'm naked, staring up at the man who has always made my heart beat faster.

"This is more like it."

He grins at that, but I pout as I realize he's still not taking off his clothes. Instead, he kisses me again, our tongues twining together intimately as I slide my legs around him, rubbing against him.

He turns his attention to my breasts, kissing his way across them before taking one of my nipples in his mouth. I sigh as he sucks and plays, driving me crazy with anticipation.

He kisses along the white scar above my breast, his brow lowering. Then he slowly makes his way down, until he's staring at the red scar near my right hip. He shudders, pressing his lips against it for a long moment.

I sigh, burying my fingers in his hair as he moves on, brushing the scruff of his cheek against my lower belly in a way that makes me giggle.

He does it again, grinning up at me. "I love your laugh."

I can feel his need for me as he moves lower again, his tongue probing me as I let out a moan. He continues to suck and lick, driving me crazy until I'm shattering in his arms.

He simply slides his hands beneath my butt, lifting me closer to his mouth. "I'm not done."

I gasp as he buries his tongue deeper before moving up to my clit, where he strokes, driving me out of my mind. He slides one of his hands free and enters me with one large finger, letting out a rough laugh as I clamp down around him, my muscles turning languid with ecstasy.

He makes me come three more times, until I'm exhausted, trembling in his arms.

"Now you," I slur as he lies down, lifting me until I'm curled against his chest.

He laughs. "We have plenty of time, my love. Go to sleep."

CHAPTER EIGHTEEN

Vivian

"Are you sure you want to go through with this?" Sarissa asks me, a smile playing around her mouth.

I laugh, giddy with happiness. "I'm surer than I've ever been of anything in my life."

Cauri shoots Sarissa a look, and I hide a smile. There's still no love lost between them. I wish my friends could have been here for this, but unlike Beth, I'm not willing to wait to make things official. And even if I were, my alien king wouldn't hear of it.

Mating ceremonies are different on this side of the water. First, there's no fire. Second, this will be my coronation as well. Even without the threat of the Dokhalls and the Zintas, I wouldn't have expected the other women to make the journey. Ellie still hasn't had her baby, and I know I'm not the only one who is starting to get worried.

At least Sarissa is here. And while she jokes about me being a runaway bride, I know she's happy for me.

I've never imagined getting married on Earth. I'd never met anyone who made me even remotely close to imagining wearing a big white dress and walking down an aisle. Maybe that's why I've gone with pure, unrelenting black.

I gaze at my reflection in the mirror, and even I have to admit I look great. The material of my dress is so fine that it almost reminds me of cobwebs, draped over a silky under-layer. Tiny jewels catch the light when I move, and the dress hugs every inch of my body without being at all lewd.

Arix added to my new jewelry collection while I was still recovering. The jewels are jet black, an obsidian so dark that I wanted to stroke them while murmuring "my precious." Each jewel is wrapped in a fine silver nest, allowing hints of onyx to peek out each time it hits the light.

He murmured in my ear, calling me his dark queen as he fastened the necklace around my throat, handing me the earrings to try on. I smile. I can't wait to see the look on his face when he sees me in this getup.

I blow out a nervous breath and glance over my shoulder at Sarissa. She's wearing crimson red, some of her long blonde hair pinned slightly back off her face, the rest a sheet of silk down her back. I sent a message to Rakiz's camp, explaining we have the chip, but Dragix still isn't back from his hunting trip. My cousin is getting impatient, and I know damn well if Dragix doesn't appear soon, she's going to take the trip across the water by herself.

I offered to send her with a group of guards, but she refused, saying that even if she did trust Arix's guards after everything we've been through, traveling in a group would attract too much attention. I have to admit she's got a point. That doesn't mean I'm going to let her go alone though. She narrows her eyes at me as if reading my mind.

"You're becoming a queen today, V. Let's focus on that."

I frown. "I just don't get why you can't get Dragix to pick you up so you can deliver the chip to Alexis."

She laughs. "Well, the dragon may have been acting as a flying taxi when everyone thought you'd die, but he's actually kind of an important asset in this war."

I stare at her, and she sighs. "He's tracking a group of Zintas who decided to take their chances with the Dokhalls. Arix gave him their scents, and he's going to take them out."

It makes sense. The Dokhalls' weapons make them more of a threat, but the Zintas know this planet. They know who's allied with who, where the Dokhalls are most likely to be in danger, and how to evade Dragix's excellent nose. Spoiler alert: it involves covering themselves with dirt and poop.

Keeping the Zintas from allying with the Dokhalls could be critical in winning this war.

Sarissa leans against the wall. "We said we'd talk about this later, Viv. This is your mating ceremony. You need to focus on yourself."

I open my mouth, but Cauri tuts, sliding one last jeweled pin into my hair. Unlike the usual complicated updo, this style is relatively simple by design. After all, I need to leave enough room for my crown. My stomach flutters at the thought, and all I can hear is my mother's voice in my head.

She didn't even think I was smart enough to go to college; what would she say if she knew I was about to help rule a kingdom? And I *will* be ruling. Arix made it clear I will be more than just a figurehead.

"I would be an idiot if I didn't use your conniving, brilliant, resourceful brain," he told me. "And I am many things, but I am not an idiot." I may not have much faith in myself, but apparently, Arix has enough faith for both of us.

Cauri steps away, pronouncing me ready. I get to my feet, and Sarissa gives me a shaky smile. "You look beautiful," she says. "You're gonna be one hell of a queen, cuz."

I blink back tears, and she laughs, wrapping me in a bear hug. "I'm going to go take my place downstairs," she says. "Unless you need me to help you make a quick getaway?" She raises her eyebrow, her eyes laughing at me, and I shake my head.

"Thanks for being so good about this."

"Hey, you want to rule a kingdom on an alien planet? Who am I to get in your way?" She winks at me and then saunters out the door, likely about to make every man waiting in the ballroom downstairs swallow his tongue. Well, every man except one, I hope.

I take one last glance in the mirror and nod. Cauri smiles at me, and her hard face is suddenly beautiful. "I was the queen's maid, you know," she murmurs. "She loved her mate and her son more than anything. She never treated me like just a maid. We were close friends, and when she died, I swore I'd help protect her boy. Kilza would like you. She also had a quick wit and a smart mouth, although not many people got to see it. She was brave too. She'd be so proud of both of you."

This time, a tear escapes my eye, and Cauri shakes her head in mock disapproval before wiping it away. "Your king is waiting for you," she says, and I nod.

"I'm ready."

She smiles at me again, and I feel a little like I'm in the twilight zone. I'm tempted to ask her if she's drunk, but ever since I nearly died and she saw exactly what it did to Arix, she's been surprisingly nice. In fact, she hasn't called me a trollop once. The last time my contraceptive tonic arrived, she remarked that I surely wouldn't need it for much longer.

It's more than a little weird.

I make my way downstairs, feeling like I'm floating on air. While the dinner, dancing, and general festivities will take place in the grand ballroom, the first part of the ceremony will be in the throne room.

I suck in a breath as I arrive, and the guards on either side of the doors throw them open, revealing the room itself, which is packed with more people than I could've imagined.

But my gaze goes past them to Arix. He's dressed formally, wearing a black crown, and his midnight-blue eyes are burning into mine as if I'm the only thing he sees.

The feeling is mutual.

Our eyes stay locked together as I walk toward him. I may have been nervous until I saw him, but now I'm consumed with joy and delight.

I feel as if every single moment of my life has been leading to this one. Korzyn stands on Arix's left, and my mind flashes back to the first time I saw Arix, in this very room. I was so nervous, wondering if we could trust him, and yet I was intrigued and hopelessly attracted despite myself.

I come to a stop in front of him, and we share a grin. I don't know about him, but I feel as if we've gotten away with something. After all, neither of us is dead, and instead, we get our very own happily ever after.

The commander steps close, turning to a guard who presents him with a cushion. My stomach flushes at the sight of the crown on that cushion, and I catch Sarissa's eye. She grins at me, giving me a tiny thumbs-up, and I almost laugh.

The commander takes the crown, and I bow my head.

Arix's voice washes over me. Somehow still low and intimate even as it carries over the crowd. "Do you, Vivian, swear to give your life to your king, your people, and your crown?"

"I swear." The crown is heavier than I ever imagined, but I manage to lift my head without it falling off, and I count that as a win as the crowd cheers.

I meet Arix's gaze, and I blink back tears at the joy I see there. After everything he's been through, he deserves whatever happiness he can find, and I'm the lucky girl who gets to give it to him.

He leans down and takes my mouth, and from the gasps that sound, I'm guessing this is rather unusual.

And from the way his hands cup my face, I'm guessing he doesn't care.

I laugh against his mouth, and he pulls back, grinning at me. "Congratulations, Your Majesty."

I blink at the title, and he offers me his hand, leading me from the throne room.

And to the beginning of the rest of our lives.

EPILOGUE

V ivian

I give the man sitting in the corner of the room my most flirtatious smile, tilting my head so more of my hair falls over my naked breast.

I've been planning this surprise since before everything went down at the banquet. When I told my cousin what I was going to do, she high-fived me, saying I was sly as a fox and obviously, I'd found my lady balls.

Come to think of it, that could mean this is a really bad idea.

It's too late to even check in with Sarissa now. She left to take the chip to Alexis a few days ago, Korzyn by her side.

"You're frowning again."

"Sorry."

I had to lock Cauri out, since I know damn well she'd lose her mind if she found out exactly what I'm up to in here.

Arix is away, negotiating with another tribe king. Since he'll only be gone for the day, I told him I'd stay here. He narrowed his eyes at me suspiciously, knowing I don't like to be left behind ever.

FOMO is real.

But this is the perfect opportunity to get this taken care of, before my possessive king comes back.

The door slams open, and Arix walks in.

He takes one look at my undressed state and the male sitting in the corner of the room, and a roar leaves his throat.

Uh-oh.

I jump to my feet, wrapping the blanket around me as he advances on the painter.

His guards burst through the door, and he whirls on them.

"Out!"

My mouth goes dry. "Arix, I can explain."

"Explain what, lovely? How I open up to you and find you mostly naked and alone in *my* rooms with another male?"

"You were supposed to be away this afternoon!"

He growls. Then he turns from me, advancing toward the artist, who is currently cowering in the corner.

I jump in front of him. "This was a surprise for you, you giant asshole!"

He stares at me. "Consider me surprised."

I roll my eyes. Men. I move toward the easel, but Arix catches my arm.

"No closer."

I break his hold the way Hewex once taught me. "We've been working on this for days! We were almost done, and now you've ruined it."

"*Days?*" He gapes at me, and then his eyes turn to ice as he returns his attention to the artist in the corner.

I stalk toward the easel, avoiding the hand Arix shoots out toward me. I turn it, revealing the painting.

"You said you wanted one of my 'photographs.' This is the closest I could manage. You're fucking welcome."

I turn to stride away, but Arix clamps his arm around my waist, holding me to him and ignoring my struggles as he examines the painting.

"For me?"

"Of course it's for you!"

He glances at the artist, who is currently attempting to mold his body into the stone wall behind him.

"This is incredible."

"Th-thank you, Your Majesty."

He's right. The artist has captured the dark red of the blanket I hold in front of me, barely covering one breast. My hair is thrown over my shoulder, covering the other. One of my legs is bare on the bed, the other hidden by the blanket mounded between my legs. I'm wearing the jewelry Arix gave me and nothing else. Just as he wanted.

The arm clamped around my waist softens slightly but not enough for me to escape.

"For me?" he asks again, and some of the fury leaves me at the wonder in his voice. This king can afford anything he wants. But when was the last time someone gave him a gift? Something tells me it was probably back when his parents were alive.

"Yes."

He glances down at me, and I almost flinch at the emotion in his eyes. He gently brushes his mouth against mine and then turns to the artist, who still looks as if he's worried he might be dragged away in chains at any moment.

"This is amazing. Thank you, and I apologize for my reaction."

I blink. Arix is apologizing? People must be ice skating in hell.

"You're...welcome, Your Majesty."

"How much longer until this is finished?"

"One more sitting, Your Majesty. The finishing touches I can do alone."

Arix nods. "You will be rewarded handsomely for this. I will ensure it. Please return tomorrow for the last sitting."

The artist smiles, leaving his paints where they are and scurrying toward the door.

Arix watches him go. Then he examines the painting some more, ignoring me as I wiggle against him.

"This is an incredible gift," he says. "While I don't appreciate another male seeing you like this, I will hang this in front of my bed, where I can appreciate it." He drags his gaze away from the painting and brushes my hair off my face. "Thank you."

I frown at him, still unwilling to let him off the hook after that reaction. "What exactly did you think was going on here?"

"I didn't think," he admits. "I saw you looking like all my fantasies come to life, with another male staring at you intently. And I lost my mind. I'm sorry."

Two apologies in one day. Wow.

I sigh. "I guess I understand. I should've told you about it, but I wanted it to be a surprise."

"It was definitely a surprise," he says. His eyes heat as he stares at the jewels circling my neck and dangling from my ears. "We are still learning each other. I promise I will work to be the male who deserves you."

"A male who doesn't jump to conclusions?"

He looks remorseful at that, and I laugh. He studies the painting some more before sending me a wicked smile in return. "Now drop that blanket so I can thank you properly."

Arix spends all night thanking me properly. In the morning, I groan at a knock on the door, burying my head under the covers. Next to me, Arix laughs. He's not usually a morning person, but satisfaction is rolling off him in waves this morning.

After the way he made me scream his name last night, I can't really blame him.

Arix pats me on the butt and rolls out of bed, wrapping a blanket around his waist. He opens the door, and I can practically hear the frown in his voice.

"Pexor," he murmurs, and I sit up out of sight.

"I'm sorry to disturb you, Your Majesty."

"From the look on your face, you're not bringing good news."

"It's the commander, Your Majesty."

I get out of bed at that, reaching for my dress. Arix flicks me a glance, waiting until I'm dressed before he waves Pexor in.

"What about the commander?" I ask, my pulse racing. Sarissa. Oh God, what if something's happened to Sarissa?

"One of the cooks was working with your enemies, Your Majesty. One of the other cooks found poison at her workstation."

Arix's expression is terrible. "What has she said so far?"

Pexor sighs. "She has been taken to the dungeons. But she was the cook in charge of preparing the commander's food for this trip."

I step forward. "Korzyn isn't stupid, right? Didn't you say he's one of the most paranoid people you know?"

Arix wraps his arm around my shoulders, pulling me

close. "He's paranoid about *my* safety. Right now, he's focused on keeping your cousin alive. He won't be expecting to be targeted himself."

I rub my arms, suddenly freezing. "Why would they target him? There's no point."

He shrugs. "Revenge, perhaps. The commander has insisted I have people taste my food ever since I took the throne. There was no way anyone could target me through my food and get away with it. They would likely find it ironic to kill my commander."

"We have to find them."

Arix nods. "I will get messages to all our allies on that side of the water." He turns to Pexor. "Begin drafting those messages and ensuring we have warriors ready to travel today."

Panic makes my hands shake. But beneath the panic is warmth. Comfort. Because whatever I face next, I'll face it with this man at my side. And that means I can face anything.

Arix obviously takes my silence as worry, because he takes my hands in his, pressing his lips to the knuckles on each of my hands. "If we have to, we'll go after them ourselves. We'll find them. I promise you."

How did I get so lucky?

"I love you," I murmur, and I can't help but laugh as Arix points toward the door and Pexor hightails it out of our rooms.

"I love you too," he purrs. "How about I show you just how much?"

I squeal as he lifts me into his arms, marching back toward his bed.

The End

Thank you for reading Enticed by the Alien Warrior! I had so much fun writing Vivian and Arix- two people who were still reeling from the events of their past, and determined not to allow anyone close enough to hurt them again.

Next up is Sarissa's story in Conquered by the Alien Warrior. Conquered is the final book in the Warriors of Agron series, however many of the women who landed in the second ship are appearing in my new series titled Society of Savages. Book one releases in May 2021.

Want to be the first to know about the spin-off series and any future deals and updates? Sign up for my free newsletter here.

And don't forget to come say hi on Facebook- Hope Hart Author.

Keep reading for a sneak peek of Conquered by the Alien Warrior.

Stay safe, and happy reading x

CONQUERED BY THE ALIEN WARRIOR

Chapter One

Sarissa

I creep along the castle halls, my footsteps light and exceedingly careful. I pause, breathe, and strain my ears.

No sign of movement. Still quiet. This castle is different in the dead of the night. Torches are lit at intervals along each corridor, their flames dancing as I pass. But the obsidian stone seems to suck up all that light, spitting it back out through the thin, gleaming silver veins cutting through the stone.

Beneath my dress, I'm wearing sturdy boots—broken in by hours of walking through the castle, the town nearby, and the marketplace. Those hours of walking and talking were worth it—giving me the contacts I need to sneak out of here and back to Rakiz's camp.

I take one more step, and the hair on the back of my neck stands up.

Suddenly, I'm back at the Farm after being recruited by the CIA, listening to my favorite instructor.

I freeze.

Your intuition exists for one reason and one reason only: to keep you alive. If you don't listen to it, you're ignoring a God-given gift.

I glance around. Still quiet. Deathly quiet. *Too* quiet.

Damn it.

I can't just stand here and wait. The attack against Vivian and Arix proved there are people in this castle that can't be trusted.

Sure, those traitors might be dead. But betrayal begins as a seed of bitterness and is watered by fury. Who knows who else might still have a bone to pick with the king—and his guests?

The corridors in this wing of the castle are like a rabbit warren, with little rhyme or reason. And yet from what I know about Arix, *everything* he does has a reason. My guess is these corridors are designed to confuse anyone who shouldn't necessarily be walking in this part of the castle.

I grind my teeth and walk faster. Two more intersections to go, and then I take a right. From there, I just need to jog down several flights of stairs in the servants' quarters, and I'm—

Slam.

Something comes out of the darkness, looming in my peripheral vision. I duck, automatically twisting, but it keeps coming. I blink, and my breath leaves me in a whoosh as I'm shoved against the stone wall, inches from a flickering torch.

The light from that torch spills over the commander's face, and I curse.

He smiles at me, but there's no amusement in that smile.

It simply amplifies the sharp planes of his face. The flames reflect back at me from his silver eyes, making him look like a demon who's come to drag me down to hell.

I squirm and writhe, but he's using his weight to hold me in place against the stone, his huge body like a slab of concrete against me.

Why do these Braxian men have to be so damn big?

I scowl up at him, and his smile widens. Trust him to gloat once he has me pinned.

"What do you want?" I hiss, careful to keep my voice quiet. The last thing I need is to wake up my cousin.

"Funny thing about human females," he says, ignoring my question. "No matter how quiet you think you are, your movements sound like thunder to my ears."

I scoff. He's lying. I'm great at being sneaky. He's definitely lying.

For sure lying.

Focus, Sarissa.

I bare my teeth at him. "And why would you care?"

"Because my king has charged me with making sure you don't get killed traveling back to *your* tribe without me."

I'd love to punch the smug look off his face, but it'd make too much noise. In one sentence—and with that tone —he's told me that a) both he and the king think I'd be killed if I traveled alone and b) I belong elsewhere and I'm sure as hell not welcome here.

It pisses me off.

"Well," I say sweetly, "it's not like Arix's little lapdog can think for himself, hmm?"

I don't think he knows what a lapdog is, but from his expression, the translator in his ear has given him a pretty good idea. All hints of amusement leave his face. And then he smiles again, and the gleam of his teeth in the dark makes me shiver.

It's probably not a good idea to piss off the Braxian commander, but I can't seem to help myself.

"I was told to make sure you don't leave alone, since you seem to have problems controlling your impulses. Our enemies have been spotted in many places between this castle and Rakiz's camp, and yet you believe you can go alone?"

He curls his lip at me, and I push against his chest, but he's not budging.

"You asshole. This castle is a shitshow. Your *enemies* almost killed the king *and* my cousin. Why would I trust any of your guards to go with me when they can't even be trusted not to attempt to murder their monarch?"

Korzyn's face goes blank, and I fight back a smile. Score. As commander of Arix's army and the man tasked with keeping the king alive, it must *burn* that so many people so close to the king ended up being dirty.

To be fair, Korzyn and Arix knew about most of the traitors, and they were playing a long game, drawing out anyone who would betray them so they could solve the problem in one swoop. Unfortunately, their schemes almost cost my cousin her life, and while *she* may have moved on, to me that's an unforgivable offense.

"We've solved that problem," Korzyn grits out.

I tilt my head. "Have you?" I smirk, just because I know it pisses him off. "Have you really?"

He's silent, and I almost cheer as his jaw tightens.

Unfortunately, I don't have time to hang around here and chat. My contact is waiting for me to get on his boat.

"Look, Korzyn, I don't want to argue with you. I need to get the control chip back to Alexis so she can start working on that ship and we can get off this planet. Unfortunately, I can't trust your guards not to be working with the Dokhalls, and if they get the chip, they'll either attempt to take the ship by force or destroy the chip out of spite."

His face looks like it's carved out of granite. "I don't care."

"Excuse me?"

"I don't care who you trust. I've made a deal with Arix, and that deal includes protecting your worthless life."

I roll my eyes. "Not if I can help it."

He grins, and this time he looks genuinely amused. I attempt to ignore what it does to me to see the hard lines of his face relax, those eyes lightening.

"You can't."

I frown, but suddenly I'm spinning in place, Korzyn's hands expertly twirling me until I'm facing the wall. I slam my head back, and he curses as I make contact with his face.

The scuffle is as quick as it is brutal. Within seconds, he has my hands caught in one of his, and he's deftly tying them behind my back.

I briefly consider screaming. If Vivian saw the commander manhandling me this way, she'd lose her shit. All it would take is one of Vivian's wide-eyed glances at Arix, and he'd order Korzyn to let me go.

Unfortunately, my pride doesn't allow it. I'm trained. I'd bet on myself against almost anyone in a fight. But I let myself be trapped against this wall and distracted, allowing Korzyn to get into the perfect position to pin me.

I fight to keep my voice steady. "I'll kill you for this."

Korzyn laughs, his voice low and muffled. I'm guessing he doesn't want to risk waking up my cousin and her sugar woogams either.

"You can try."

The words are wet, and despite myself, I grin.

"Nose a little sore, Korzyn?"

He leans forward and wipes his face against my cheek.

"Ew!"

His blood is warm, and I struggle instinctively, but it's too late. My wrists are bound.

Maybe I should just suck it up and scream. I'll collect the tattered remains of my ego later. I open my mouth only to choke as Korzyn takes the opportunity to shove a piece of material into my mouth, his hands quick as he ties it.

I slam my head back again, but he's not falling for that move twice. I'll have one hell of a bruise on the back of my head already, and he now knows I'll happily ring my own bell if I have to.

He throws me over his shoulder, ignoring my "oof" as his hard muscle digs into my belly. I shift in an attempt to knee him, but he clamps his arm around my legs. Then the bastard *slaps me on the ass* with a laugh and saunters down the hall.

My eye begins to twitch. I'm about to explode from either rage or sheer mortification.

Korzyn's quarters aren't far from mine. I should've known the commander would stay close. After all, he's made sure to follow me around since the moment I got here.

Thankfully, there are no guards outside Korzyn's door. Obviously, he's decided he doesn't need them. Or maybe he doesn't trust them. Either way, I'm saved from the humiliation that would occur if anyone else witnessed this nightmare.

Korzyn throws me onto his bed, and I wiggle until I'm on my back, staring up at him. He looks very pleased with himself, and there's something dark in his eyes as he scans me, lingering on the gag in my mouth.

"I think I prefer you like this," he says, and I glare at him so hard I'm surprised his head doesn't explode from my fury alone. "Now. Let's discuss what's going to happen next."

Korzyn

When I first learned how to grip a sword, I was young. So young I could barely lift it. My trainer had little patience and less empathy, and I was expected to swing that sword for hours each day.

My hands suffered. A particularly nasty blister formed on my palm beneath my thumb. Each day after training, I would bandage it, and it would begin the healing process only to pop open the next day. Eventually, it grew so large I had to hold my sword with my nondominant hand.

Years later, when I spoke to my trainer, I asked him why he wouldn't allow us to see the healers, who had balms that would have taken the pain from our blisters.

He laughed. "Would you have learned to swing your sword this skillfully with your left hand if your right did not pain you so?"

I glowered at him and stalked away, furious at his answer.

That blister plagued me, making it impossible to use my hand. Each time it got close to healing, I would be told to pick up my sword, bursting the protective layer and producing teeth-clenching pain. Eventually, the wound became infected, and my trainer had to relent and allow the healers to treat it.

The scar is now thick—a reminder that with every wound comes a healing. A hardening.

The female currently tied up on my bed reminds me of that blister.

Each time I see her, my protective layers burst and my jaw aches from clenching my teeth.

She is a stone in my shoe.

She glowers at me, and I allow myself a few moments to enjoy the satisfaction of seeing her tied up and helpless before me.

I'm not a spiteful male. I perform my duties, protect my king, and train with my men.

But I can't ignore the gratification I feel at seeing this vindictive female at my mercy.

It makes something tighten in my stomach, and I run my gaze over her, from her flushed face, to the pale skin above her dark-gray dress, to the worn boots on her feet.

She makes a strangled sound, beating those feet against my bed, and I laugh.

From the look on her face, she's planning my murder.

A spark of interest ignites before I can dampen it. It has been many years since I was concerned with anything other than protecting Arix from the numerous attempts on his life.

"Let me tell you what will happen now," I say, and Sarissa narrows her eyes at me. They're the strangest color —neither green nor blue but somehow both at once.

"You will sleep in here, as you can't be trusted not to attempt to sneak out of this castle and I need to rest before our journey."

Her eyes flash at me, and I can't help but grin. I haven't felt this light for days.

"That's correct. I'm going with you. We leave at dawn, so I suggest you get some sleep."

She gives me a look so scathing that if I were a lesser male, I would wither under it.

"If you agree not to scream, I will remove your gag. Not that anyone would come for you, but it's time for me to rest."

She nods, and I lean forward. Her legs tremble, her feet twitching as if she is fighting the impulse to kick me in the head, and I almost smile. This female is not stupid. If she knocks me out, she will be stuck in this room, gagged and bound, until I awake. And then I will be furious.

"Look," she says when I untie the gag, "why don't you just tell Arix you went to get me but I'd already escaped?"

Her tone is cajoling, as if she's attempting to reason with me, and I almost laugh.

Instead, I slowly shake my head. "No. I have made a deal with Arix. If I take you back to Rakiz's camp, he'll give me something I very much want."

Her eyes sharpen with interest. "And what do you want?"

"That doesn't concern you."

Her lips thin, and her ire makes my shoulders lighten with amusement.

"I can't sleep like this," she says.

"Too bad."

"Korzyn. My hands will be damaged if I sleep with them like this. This rope is cutting off my circulation."

I'm not an idiot. She's hoping I will free her and she will somehow escape. However, Vivian will be upset if her cousin is damaged, and when Vivian is upset, Arix is enraged.

"Roll onto your side."

She thinks about it for a moment but finally complies. Her tiny feet shift, likely as she again debates whether to kick me, and I feel the strangest urge to...laugh.

She huffs out a breath as she turns over, and I take

another long piece of material, tying it around her right wrist.

"Make a fist."

She does, letting out a snort when I loosen it slightly.

"Have a lot of experience tying up women, baby?" The human endearment is heavy with sarcasm, and I grit my teeth.

"If there was ever a female who deserved to be tied to a male's bed, it's you."

She lets out a strangled noise, and I push her onto her front, enjoying her muffled growl. I tie the other end of her new tether to my bedpost before removing the cloth tying her hands together. Since I'm a merciful male, I allow her to have one hand free so she can sleep easier.

I withdraw as she flips onto her back. She glances up at where the material is attached to my bed and again rolls her eyes.

I study her face. She seems entirely too calm.

"Where are your weapons?" I ask.

"Hmm?"

From the lift of her eyebrow, she's attempting to pretend indifference. That means the female probably has at least one knife hidden somewhere. A knife she would likely use to free herself before castrating me in retaliation.

I smile. "You know, the guards are still talking about the way your cousin killed Bevix. A poisoned dagger. Brutal yet elegant. Not only did she get the poison in his bloodstream, but Arix said the way she threw that knife at his throat was a thing of beauty."

Pride flashes in Sarissa's eyes. "Vivian has always had exceptionally good aim."

My smile widens. "You know what I found most interesting about that?"

"I'm sure you're going to tell me."

"No one knew she had a knife. Otherwise, our enemies would have taken it from her."

From the rage burning in the hellion's eyes, she knows exactly what's going to happen next. She lets out a shriek, and when I push up her dress, this time she does kick out.

I freeze. Her thighs are pale, toned, and ridiculously smooth. But from her knees down, long scars trail across her shins, onto the tops of her feet.

"What happened here?" The long white scars wind around her legs like ropes. A small part of me pities her. The pain must have been excruciating.

"None of your business."

Her other hand is free, and she aims it at my head, growling when I catch it.

"Let me go, perv."

I smile at the sheath strapped to her thigh. "Is this knife dipped in poison?"

"You'll find out when you least expect it," she vows, and I laugh.

She stares at me, likely unused to hearing me make such a sound. Truthfully, I'm also unused to making it.

"Where are your other weapons?"

She clamps her mouth shut, and I sigh. I check her boots next, encountering not one but two small daggers. I run my hands up her arms, finding another knife. I frown at the long piece of metal wrapped around her upper arm.

"Jewelry," she tells me, and I sigh, removing the metal band. While even I can admit this female is beautiful, there's no doubt she doesn't spend much time on her appearance. Her lady's maid was imprisoned after working with our enemies, and the castle gossiped relentlessly about how Sarissa refused to take another maid, choosing instead to get ready alone each day.

The only jewelry I have ever seen her wear are the blue stones in her ears. If she wants me to believe the strange piece of metal in my hand is jewelry, she'll be disappointed, because it most definitely is not.

Her eyes darken with frustration. But she stays silent.

"Is this all?"

She nods, and I sigh.

"I'm tired. Don't make me search the rest of you."

She pulls at her hand, still trapped in my fist, and I let it go with a warning look. Her hand disappears down her dress, between her breasts, and she pulls out a thin knife.

My mouth drops open. The woman is a walking armory.

She smirks at me. "I want these all back in the morning."

I study her. She's waiting for me to agree, one eyebrow raised.

"Where is the last weapon?"

She growls, gesturing at the pile next to me on the bed. "Are you kidding me? You just took it."

I reach into the pocket of her dress, pulling out a pile of papers. One of them is a map of this part of Agron, and I study it with interest. "You've been busy."

She ignores that, and I place the papers next to her weapons.

I survey every inch of her, going as far as to make her roll onto her stomach as I run my fingers along her spine. She shivers, and I ignore what that does to my body.

"No knife here?"

"I have a bung shoulder. I can't reach for it quickly."

I almost concede, but while her face is a blank mask, she can't hide the hint of triumph in her eyes as I begin gathering her weapons.

I lean forward and pull the ornate pin from her hair. Her golden locks tumble down around her face, and this time, she's truly furious.

I study the hairpin, unsheathing it and whistling as I poke the sharp end. "I haven't seen these before."

"I had it made for me," she grits out.

I meet her eyes. "I wouldn't have known, but you rarely wear ornaments in your hair."

I don't know why I feel the need to explain, but she's silent as I move her weapons away. I'd think her cowed if not for the resentment that burns in her eyes.

"You will rue the fucking day you decided to come after me. Do you hear me?"

I smile at that, placing her weapons on the table by my window.

Sarissa keeps talking. "I bet taking my weapons and tying me up makes you feel like a man."

I scowl at that. This female has an uncanny ability to annoy me, which she uses ruthlessly. And I usually can't help but retaliate.

I pick up another piece of material, ignoring her gasp of outrage as I take her free hand. She bucks, kicking out, and I narrowly miss her foot as she aims at my balls.

Vicious female.

I tie her other hand to my bed. Turns out I'm not a merciful male after all.

"You're right," I say. "It does make me feel like a man."

She stays sullenly silent, and I sigh, pulling one of my blankets from the bed. I leave the rest for the hellion and walk toward the long sofa in front of my fire. She casts the flames a wary look, and I frown at her.

"Go to sleep."

Click here to read Conquered by the Alien Warrior.

ALSO BY HOPE HART

The Arcav Alien Invasion Series

The Arcav King's Mate

The Arcav Commander's Human

The Arcav General's Woman

The Arcav Prince's Captive

A Very Arcav Christmas

The Arcav Captain's Queen

The Arcav Guard's Female

The Warriors of Agron Series

Taken by the Alien Warrior

Claimed by the Alien Warrior

Saved by the Alien Warrior

Seduced by the Alien Warrior

Protected by the Alien Warrior

Captured by the Alien Warrior

Rescued by the Alien Warrior

Enticed by the Alien Warrior

Conquered by the Alien Warrior

www.ingramcontent.com/pod-product-compliance
Lightning Source LLC
Chambersburg PA
CBHW051221210726
48290CB00003B/735